The
Illusionist

By
Fran Heckrotte

THE ILLUSIONIST
© 2006 BY FRAN HECKROTTE

ISBN: 978-1-933113-31-9

CREDITS

EXECUTIVE EDITOR: TARA YOUNG
COVER DESIGN BY SHERI (GRAPHICARTIST2020@HOTMAIL.COM)

Published by
Intaglio Publications
P O Box 357474
Gainesville, Florida 32635

Visit us on the web: www.intagliopub.com

DEDICATION

My special thanks and gratitude go to my favorite French-Canadian and writing consultant, Ms. Annabelle Lamarre, for encouraging me to put my fantasies in writing; for the hours, days, and weeks she sacrificed helping me brainstorm different ideas and creating the storyline and character development. Her assistance in translating English into French, proofreading the manuscript for the obvious errors, and critiquing the inconsistencies was invaluable, saving me time and my sanity. Most of all, she listened to my ramblings and made me believe she really enjoyed the finished product. Although Annabelle continually minimizes her role in assisting me, without her assistance, her ideas, and her encouragement, this novel would not exist.

ACKNOWLEDGMENTS

Special thanks To my friends, Remy, Scamper, Tess, Blaize, and Laurie, who are also my beta readers. They took their time to read the story, share their thoughts, and encourage me to have the story published.

My thanks to Kathy Smith from Intaglio Publications for taking a chance in making this publication a reality and for her patience while working with an inexperienced author. Sheri Dragon, thank you for your extraordinary artwork on the cover.

To Tara Young: Thanks isn't enough for the hard job of editing, her suggestions, her patience, and skillful expertise.

And finally, to Howie, who hasn't a clue as to why I'm thanking him but is sure to ask once he finds out his name was mentioned.

Chapter One

Soft gray swirls of mist drifted across the stage like the fog from an old Boris Karloff movie. A chill spread through the restless crowd as it waited impatiently for the show to begin. The appearance of a shadowy figure moving toward them brought an eerie silence to the makeshift amphitheater.

Tall with dark flowing hair, the costumed figure walked slowly out of the mist and into the light. Blue leather slacks, a white satin blouse unbuttoned at the collar, and a silver sequined vest emphasized the lithe figure of the mysterious woman. The face framed with short bangs and long black hair was partially hidden behind a matching silver and blue leather mask. High cheekbones, full red lips, and a chiseled jaw provided tantalizing hints of the woman's beauty and strength. The lips, which were faintly turned up at the corners, smiled warmly at the audience before opening to display even white teeth—with two exceptions. Slightly elongated, her canine teeth emphasized the almost animalistic aura surrounding the Illusionist.

Pale, icy blue eyes peered intently through narrow slits and stared coolly at the audience. The silence continued. She tilted her head slightly, her eyes slowly scanning the crowd. Every seat was filled, and a few people were leaning against the walls at the back of the large room.

Motioning for an attendant, she leaned down and whispered something in the young woman's ear. Immediately, the attendant scurried off, signaling for two ushers to follow her. Within minutes, several people arrived carrying fold-up chairs. Once everyone was seated, the

Illusionist nodded her thanks and focused her attention on the audience. Raising both arms in the air, she spoke softly into the collar mic.

"Good evening, ladies and gentlemen."

Her voice was like the husky whisper of a seductress, beckoning to each listener, drawing the audience unconsciously forward in their seats, ears craving to hear the next word. A faint accent caressed each syllable with an exoticness of uncertain origin.

"Thank you for coming to the performance this evening. I am Yemaya. I hope everyone here will find tonight's show interesting and memorable. Most of you probably do not know about my namesake. Yemaya is the West African creation goddess. She is believed to be the goddess of the moon, the oceans, and the colors of blue and silver. I have chosen to make them my own for this particular event for obvious reasons."

The Illusionist strolled across the length of the stage, twirling a couple of times to display the beautifully tailored silver and blue outfit.

"Tonight's show honors the goddess and her creations. My crew and I plan on giving you an evening you will not forget for a long time. If, however, anyone is dissatisfied, please tell the young woman at the admission booth, and she will take your name and address. Your admission fee will be returned without question. Now my attendant has given me a signal there will be a slight delay, so before we start the show, there are a few facts I think you should know about this place. Thank you, Suzanne."

Pivoting slightly, she motioned for two assistants to open the curtains behind her, revealing an enormous sea aquarium with a nine-foot-by-twenty-foot picture window.

"First, I would like to thank the city of Charleston and especially the staff at this beautiful ocean display for providing the facilities for my performance. It took a lot of hard work to convert this area into a mini-theater. We have placed cameras at the deep view window, which is made of a special acrylic glass. My technicians have installed large display screens in each corner of the room so everyone will have unobstructed views of the entire aquarium and of me. After all, what would the show be without a hostess?" She laughed softly. "Okay, Suzanne says I can start earning that $500 admission fee you just paid. One last thing. The resident sea life here has been moved to another location for the evening. You will understand why shortly. Now I direct your attention to that far corner of the aquarium."

All eyes followed the direction she was pointing. Slowly, a semi-transparent door slid sideways, exposing a dark chamber.

"Behold, Shezara, the main reason no cameras have been allowed in here. Any flash could agitate her, and she is *not* an animal we want agitated. Beautiful, is she not?" Yemaya exclaimed, sweeping her right arm toward the chamber. When nothing happened, the crowd groaned, some sitting back in their seats. Laughing, she turned back to the audience.

"Well, it seems Shezara is bashful tonight. Perhaps we can entice her out." Motioning to an assistant, Yemaya backed to the right side of the stage, allowing the young woman dressed in gray access to the steps leading to the top edge of the glass. In her hands was a large platter, covered by a dark red cloth. Climbing to the platform at the top of the steps, the assistant uncovered the platter, revealing an enormous chunk of meat and proceeded to dump it into the crystalline waters.

"Let us see if Shezara is hungry," the Illusionist chuckled. "Shezara, dinner time!" Yemaya called, turning toward the window to tap on the thick transparent barrier separating her and the enormous fish.

Again the crowd leaned forward in anticipation, only to jerk back in their seats. From the depths of the darkened chamber, almost faster than the eye could follow, an enormous shark surged toward the meat. Mouth open, thousands of razor sharp teeth glistening under the lights, the creature scooped up the meat, swallowed, then turned her enormous length away from the glass, missing it by a mere meter. Cruising back to the far side, she swam lazily up and down the length of the glass searching for more food.

"Ah, Shezara, my friend, I sense your need. Perhaps I can help alleviate the hunger," Yemaya whispered, her hand gently caressing the glass before walking back to center stage. She let her eyes wander over the audience, assuring herself she had everyone's complete attention. Noticing a young woman in the fifth row, her gaze lingered for a few moments.

So I see you've returned, she thought, her icy blue eyes gleaming brightly. *Perhaps tonight you will have your answers, perhaps not. We will see.*

Dakota Devereaux pulled out her pad and pencil, scribbling down the evening's events. Whether from the excitement or plain bad luck, the tip of the pencil snapped, poking a small hole in the page. Cursing, she dug in her small handbag for something else to write with. Dakota sighed with relief when she found a ballpoint pen at the bottom. It was critical she not miss anything. Later she would compare what she witnessed that evening with the other five shows. Halfway through the first word, the ink pen began skipping.

"Damn! Damn! Damn!" she muttered, unaware others had turned to look at her. Placing the tip of the pen between her lips, she sucked hard, trying to get the ink to flow. With her lips puckered around the tip, cheeks sunken in, she felt the silence surrounding her.

She looked up to find several people staring at her in amusement. Quickly, she looked toward the stage, only to lock gazes with the pale blue behind the mask. Dark green eyes widened momentarily from shock and embarrassment and something else—something she couldn't quite describe. Dakota quickly pulled the pen from her mouth, neutralized her expression, and glanced down at her notepad, muttering under her breath.

With a slight smirk, Yemaya turned her attention back to the audience who had been caught up in the silent exchange between the two women.

"Ladies and gentlemen, again, I would like to introduce you to Shezara, a twelve-foot great white shark, the only one of this size in captivity. She belongs to the largest species of fish on the planet. I am sure everyone is aware of the damage great whites can do. At twelve feet, she is considered an average-size female. I would hate to see a large one," the Illusionist joked. "Now before I begin my illusion, does anyone have any questions? I will try to answer them, but I warn you—my personal life is personal, and I will not reveal secrets of the trade."

"That doesn't leave much, now does it?" an older gentleman in the audience grumbled.

"That would depend," she mocked softly. "Now who has the first question?"

Looking around, Yemaya noticed a small hand waving tentatively from the seventh row. Pointing to the child, she smiled.

"Hello, what is your name?"

"Sandy," the little girl answered shyly.

"Well, Sandy, what would you like to know?"

"Well, um...do you have any kids?"

"Sandy, Sandy, Sandy," the Illusionist laughed. "Now I just said no personal questions."

"But that's not personal, Ms. Yemaya. Kids ain't personal, you know," she explained seriously. "Almost everyone has them, so how can that be personal?"

Pretending to think about the answer, Yemaya nodded sagely.

"You know, Sandy, you have me there. With so many kids around, how can it be personal? So, no. No kids."

"That's too bad," Sandy responded sadly.

"Now why is that?" Yemaya asked, curious about the response.

"Well, you see, you're such a pretty lady for being so old, and you seem real nice, too."

Looking indignant, Yemaya placed her hands on her hips and leaned forward.

"Old? Just how old do you think I am, young lady?"

Blushing, the girl hid her face behind her hands and mumbled.

"Sandy, I could not hear you. How old do you think I am?"

"Um...mommy says you have to be *at least* thirty," Sandy replied, peeking between her fingers.

"Thirty, huh?"

Turning to look at the woman sitting next to the child, Yemaya chuckled as the highly embarrassed mother sank low in her chair, her eyes turned down in an attempt to avoid the penetrating blue gaze.

"Well, thank you, *Mom*. I never considered thirty to be old. In fact, I would consider it quite young," she responded seriously. "Now any other questions?" She turned back toward the audience, the issue of age unanswered.

"Yeah, I got one," a male voice yelled from the shadows. "How'd you get to be a *magician*?" The sarcasm penetrated the darkness, causing several heads to turn to identify the annoying individual.

Crossing her arms, Yemaya ignored the urge to punish the man for his ignorance. The angry stares of her audience spoke eloquently for her.

"I am not a magician. Magicians deal with magical powers. I am an illusionist. No sleight of hand, no pulling rabbits from a hat, no cutting people in half and putting them back together again. I do not possess the skills to create the tricks a magician must to entertain the public. I merely make things appear or disappear. I create a dilemma for you to figure out. How I do it is up to you to discover," she stated cooly.

As the evening went on, the Illusionist continued to answer questions and asked a few of her own.

"Unfortunately, I have to call a halt to the questions to start the show. Shezara is restless. One of my assistants is about to place some of her favorite food in the aquarium. This should whet her appetite, making her extremely hungry. I will then enter the water. If Shezara follows her normal instincts, she will charge me, mouth open. Her large size makes her quite capable of swallowing me whole, which is not my intention, I can assure you, especially since I have an appointment after the show," she joked. "If all goes as planned, one of us will disappear—hopefully me, by choice. Of course, if I am wrong, she will not be hungry for a few days and I will miss that appointment. Now please excuse me while I change into something a little more suitable for the water. Please sit back and relax until I return."

Walking off stage, Yemaya glanced again at the blonde in the fifth row. Apparently, she had found something to write with since she was again scribbling rapidly on her pad. Glancing up from her notes, Dakota's green eyes collided with those of the masked woman. Embarrassed at having been caught a second time, she quickly slid the tablet into her purse, sat back in the seat, and crossed her arms, assuming a nonchalant pose. Dakota stared unblinkingly at the entertainer, desperately hoping the dimly lit room hid her flushed cheeks. She suddenly had a feeling the woman knew more about her than she did the Illusionist.

For the first time in years, Yemaya also felt uncomfortable. This woman bothered her. She had noticed her at other performances, and each time, the young woman was taking notes. At $500 a seat, three shows cost too much for mere entertainment, unless of course, the woman was wealthy. Yemaya knew she was a journalist. What she didn't know, though, was why the petite blonde made her uneasy. She certainly wasn't a threat to her nor would she be able to uncover any details about her past. Yemaya's history had been masked from prying eyes, allowing for only a minimum paper trail, enough to satisfy the interest of most of the public. She was aware that her files had been accessed by several people over the last few months. Some were merely curious, others were journalists. A few, however, were dangerous and needed to be carefully monitored.

Putting those thoughts aside, Yemaya nodded to the woman before disappearing behind the curtains.

Once Yemaya was out of sight, Dakota exhaled deeply, her hands trembling slightly. Eye contact with the performer had been unnerving enough the first time. Two times in one night was eerie. She had followed the Illusionist for months, trying to gather information. At first, she just wanted to write an exposé on magicians and illusionists, specifically the differences in attitudes and themes.

After attending a few performances by Siegfried and Roy, David Copperfield, and a few lesser-known entertainers, she had enough data to write the article for her magazine. It was only after seeing an editorial in a prominent New York paper about Yemaya Lysanne that she decided to add one more magician/illusionist to her report.

From the moment the woman stepped on stage, Dakota was hooked. Her sheer beauty was breathtaking. Approximately six feet tall with long dark hair and eyes almost colorless with a hint of the silvery blueness of a glacial lake and the athletic build of a tri-athlete, she epitomized what every man wanted, most women wanted to be, and everyone secretly desired. After watching the performance, which left her—and everyone else—mystified,

Dakota immediately called her boss to report her discovery and to ask for an extension and additional funds.

Because of the high cost of the tickets, it took a bit of persuasion to convince Johnson to front the money to continue her research. She finally emailed him several reviews, which had recently appeared in the well-known *Magician's Magazine* and a few trade journals, along with a press release photo of her in costume, before he agreed to her request. Dakota suspected the photo was the deciding factor. Who could resist a good mystery, especially such a stunning one?

And Yemaya was exactly that. No amount of investigative research had turned up anything significant about her background. Her tax records were sealed, an unusual procedure for a foreigner. It was obvious Yemaya had powerful connections everywhere, even in the government.

The few facts and/or rumors Dakota had managed to dig up were vague at best. Once a show concluded, Yemaya simply "disappeared," at least that's how the stagehands described her exits from the building. Of course, it wasn't surprising, considering that was the main theme of her performances. Either she disappeared or the object of her attention vanished. Attempts to interview her or her assistants failed. She was reclusive and her assistants were closed-mouth. "No comment" was their mantra.

The truth was they hadn't a clue about Yemaya's personal life, but she paid excellent salaries with great benefits and was never verbally abusive. No matter how badly things went—and there were days when things went horribly wrong—she complimented everyone on their dedication and thanked them for trying. On the worst days, she'd send everyone home early with instructions to be back on the job at their regular time the next day. When the workers arrived the following morning, the previous day's problems were solved.

In the beginning, they used to ask Yemaya who had taken care of everything. She merely smiled, winked, and whispered, "ancient spirits," before walking away. It wasn't long before everyone believed her to have either supernatural powers or at the very least mysterious connections. No one was willing to anger whomever or whatever favored their employer.

Dakota wanted to know more. Perhaps the most intriguing fact was Yemaya's citizenship. Her passport indicated she was from Moldova, a small agricultural country near Romania. It was a poor nation with little to attract visitors or tourism. In fact, it had very little to offer its own citizens.

The crowd watched intently as a young woman climbed the stairs and stood on the Plexiglas platform. Slowly walking up and down, she appeared to be inspecting every inch of the clear substance. As she neared the edge overhanging the water, she kneeled, running her fingers across the smooth surface. Frowning, she motioned to a second attendant, who climbed the steps and knelt next to her.

The audience couldn't hear the conversation, but it was apparent something was wrong. So intent was their attention on the aides, they did not see Yemaya walk on stage dressed in a blue and silver wet suit and a blue rubber diving mask. She ran up the stairs and knelt between the two attendants. Running her fingers along the same area the attendant had been inspecting, the three conversed quietly.

No one noticed the great white arch her back nor the quick attack on the three women above her. Like a torpedo, her snout exploded through the platform, throwing pieces of Plexiglas and bodies into the aquarium. People jumped up screaming as water and chunks of plastic fell onto the stage below. The sound of teeth scraping the hard material grated on ears, sending cold shivers through their souls, primal fears overpowering modern logic.

Shezara was hungry. Startled from the impact of hitting the invisible barrier, she swam angrily toward the back of the tank where she stopped to watch her intended meal floundering in the water. Although her food was close, the sound of Plexiglas scraping the live coral and artificial rocks as it fell to the aquarium floor confused her. She had learned patience from a lifetime of hunting. Waiting for the noises to stop would not interfere with her needs, only delay the inevitable outcome.

Yemaya was as startled as her assistants when she felt the platform heave upward and shatter, throwing them into the water. Immediately, she searched for the great white. Seeing the fish hovering at the back of the aquarium, she checked to see if her two assistants were safe. One was already being pulled from the water by aides, but Suzanne, the young woman who had discovered the large crack in the Plexiglas, was sinking to the bottom, blood flowing from a head wound, the reddish stream trailing behind.

"A blama!" she swore, looking back toward Shezara. Cold, expressionless black eyes were focused on the unconscious woman. The urge to attack was strong, but something within the beast compelled her to stay still. For the moment, the shark was content to merely watch her prey sink to the aquarium floor.

Yemaya knew she didn't have much time to get her assistant out of the water. Her command would only affect the primitive mind for a few minutes. She dove, swimming rapidly toward the woman while keeping her‾attention focused on the shark. When Shezara made her move, the Illusionist would have to place herself between the shark and Suzanne.

She knew the snout is the most sensitive area on a shark and that it has lids that close over the eyes for protection once it nears a target. She could deflect its attention at least once by striking it on the nose and pushing off from the enormous body. More than once, though, was doubtful. Yemaya didn't have enough strength to cause it pain, but the blow would probably surprise the great white. After that, all bets were off. She would then have to reveal a few additional skills to the audience. Those she preferred to keep secret.

Within seconds, Yemaya had reached Suzanne. Grabbing her right arm, she swam toward the surface, powerful legs propelling her upward. Three of her attendants kneeled on a small remnant of the platform. A splash to her left made her glance around nervously. A crimson cloud spread slowly through the water as a large red chunk of meat sank to the bottom within a few feet of the shark.

Good thinking, Yemaya thought. *Hopefully, that will distract her long enough.*

Hearing the splash, Shezara looked toward the sound. The scent of blood passed through her nostrils, making her hunger intolerable. Food was not a conscious thought but a need. Flicking her powerful tail, she dove toward the meat, scooping it up and swallowing. It felt good sliding down her throat into her stomach, but it increased the craving. Another splash and another chunk fell near her. Grabbing it before it descended more than ten feet, she turned to look at the two "animals" swimming toward the surface. The morsels falling around her were tasty but not satisfying. Later she could clean up the pieces of meat, but now she wanted more—she wanted fresh, warm meat. She wanted them.

Yemaya's head and body broke through the water's surface, and she shoved Suzanne toward outstretched hands. Taking a deep breath as she grasped the edge of the platform with one hand, she heaved Suzanne's body upward. The three attendants quickly yanked the woman onto the remaining platform and handed her to the two paramedics behind them.

Next, they grabbed Yemaya's outstretched arm, pulling her body up and out of the water but not before the shark lunged in a last frantic attempt to procure her meal. Lips peeled back to expose gums, white teeth flashing brightly under the stage lights, and a mouth more than three feet in diameter opened wide. The head and jaws of the beast exited the water. A human would simply disappear through the cavernous mouth—that is, if it wasn't cut in half by the razor-sharp teeth.

Dakota watched in awe as the Illusionist dove for the unconscious woman, retrieved the limp body, and swam upward. Mesmerized and terrified by the events unfolding, her attention was temporarily distracted by a bright flash of light. Looking around, she noticed a small man with slightly balding brown hair, blue jeans, and red checkered shirt standing in the aisle near an exit, taking photos. The man lowered the camera, glanced at her nervously, frowned, and shuffled toward the exit, tucking the camera under his left arm.

"Tourist," she muttered in disgust. "Or paparazzi," she added as an afterthought.

Immediately, she turned back in time to see Yemaya push the woman onto the broken platform before reaching for the hands of her assistants. Her wrist was quickly grabbed, and she was pulled from the water just as the great white's body launched itself in her direction.

"Oh, God, please don't let this happen," Dakota prayed, horrified at the thought of the woman being injured or killed.

Yemaya felt an intense pain in her right shoulder as her body was hauled sharply onto the platform. At the same time, a burning sensation erupted in her right calf, causing her to gasp. Next, a loud splash was heard as a mountain of water inundated her and the others, causing the platform to shake and groan ominously.

"Quick, everyone off!" Yemaya yelled, shoving at the people around her. They scrambled down the steps and onto the stage where they collapsed from relief and exhaustion. The crowd, which had been eerily quiet for several minutes, erupted into cheers, and the onlookers turned to slap their neighbors on the back.

Yemaya turned toward one of the paramedics who had been standing by during the performance.

"How is Suzanne?" she asked, raking her hand tiredly through her damp hair, her voice husky from concern and pain.

"She's fine," he responded, pulling on a pair of surgical gloves. "We're taking her to the ER for a thorough checkup, then probably an overnight stay for observation. In the meantime, let me look at your leg. You've lost a lot of blood, you know."

Glancing at her right calf, she noticed blood streaming from a six-inch gash along the back side.

"Futui!" she groaned in disgust. "This is going to need stitches."

"'Fraid so, Ms. Lysanne," the paramedic chuckled, having a pretty good idea of what she had said and amused at the woman's tone. "Let me put a compression bandage on it, and we'll get you to the hospital."

"How about you just bandage it so I can send the audience home?" she suggested, looking toward the aquarium in an attempt to locate Shezara.

"I hate needles," she muttered, turning her attention toward two attendants who were busy throwing chunks of beef in the water to satiate the previously agitated fish. Apparently, it was working for the great white was swimming lazily up and down, scooping up each morsel as it rained toward her.

"Great job, kids," she yelled, waving her hand. "Give her another 150 pounds and call it a night. I can talk with the curator tomorrow and settle everything then."

Waving back, they continued dropping the meat into the water as others carried additional beef chucks up the ladder.

When the paramedic finished the wrap on her leg, he helped Yemaya to her feet. Taking her arm, he assisted her to the edge of the stage.

"Ladies and gentlemen, this is not exactly the entertainment I had in mind for you this evening. For that, I apologize. Please leave your names and addresses with any member of the staff or call in tomorrow with the information, and your money will be promptly refunded. As for my attendant, I have been assured by this young man that she is fine and will be back home by tomorrow. Of course, she will be given a few days off to recover," Yemaya joked to ease the tension.

The crowd laughed loudly, relieved everything had turned out well. No one had any intention of requesting a refund. The night had been more exciting than they could ever imagine, and there would be a great story to tell friends and families. The whole event had been spectacular in an odd sort of way.

"Now if you will excuse me, I need to get checked out myself and let this young man go back to work doing more important things than holding up an older woman like me. Right, Benny?" she added, glancing at his name tag and winking. Everyone laughed, applauding loudly.

Blushing, the paramedic could only nod as he helped the tall woman walk off stage into the shadows.

"There really is no need for an ambulance. One of my people will drive me to the hospital," Yemaya said. "Thanks for everything."

Benny would have objected but knew it was useless. Disappointed at the lost opportunity, he sighed.

"Okay, but you are coming to the hospital, right? I mean, this isn't your way of getting rid of me, is it?" he joked halfheartedly.

Smiling, Yemaya patted his shoulder. "No, I promise. I need to check on Suzanne, right? And of course, make sure your boss knows what a great job you did here. Now off with you."

Reluctantly, Benny gathered his equipment and left. The audience slowly filed out the exits. Yemaya gave a few more instructions to the staff, then motioned for her driver to follow her.

Dakota got into her small Volkswagen with the intention of going home. As she pulled out of the parking space, she decided to make a side trip to the hospital. There was a possibility she might be able to get information from someone there or even a short interview with Yemaya. At least it couldn't hurt to try.

Chapter Two

When Yemaya walked into the ER, she noticed the same woman who had been sitting in the fifth aisle. Unaware of Yemaya's presence, the reporter reviewed some of the notes she had jotted in her tablet, intent on being accurate with the earlier events and times. She had managed to borrow a pencil from one of the nurses. Leaning back in the chair, Dakota closed her eyes, replaying the evening over in her mind as it had unfolded. If only she had taken her cell phone. The built-in camera would have come in handy.

The thought reminded her of the strange man taking pictures. He seemed nervous when she looked at him. In fact, he left so quickly, it made her wonder if there wasn't more to him than she initially thought. Security had placed restrictions against cameras and electronic equipment inside the building, which was why she hadn't taken her phone. That would certainly account for his discomfort. Everyone had to pass through a metal detector before entering the showroom. How did he get his past security? Dakota frowned. There were more questions than answers at the moment.

A warm breath caressed her ear as she heard the soft whisper.

"Something bothering you?"

Opening her eyes, she blinked quickly at the face inches away. Pale blue eyes gleamed mischievously into her own. Dakota felt as if she were drowning in an icy lake.

"Uh...yeah...I mean, no...not really," Dakota stuttered. "Well, maybe. I don't know," she stammered, swallowing nervously.

Laughing, Yemaya straightened up and moved back a step.

"Well, you certainly covered all the avenues with that answer," she smirked. "Is it yeah, no, or maybe?" She raised her left eyebrow.

Chuckling, Dakota stood up too quickly, bumping into the taller woman.

"Oh, gosh. Sorry. You okay?"

"Yes, no problem."

"That's good. I can be so clumsy sometimes. Anyway, to answer your question...all three, I guess," she chuckled. "Hi, I'm Dakota. It's an honor to meet you, Ms. Lysanne." She extended her right hand.

Yemaya continued looking into Dakota's green eyes as she took the hand firmly in her own. When she first entered the emergency room, she had noticed Dakota sitting in the corner, her head back and eyes shut. Yemaya's first instinct was to slip quietly past her, get the leg tended to, then slip out unnoticed. But the woman intrigued her and now was as good an opportunity as any to find out who she was.

"Drop the Ms., please. My name is Yemaya. So, Dakota. That is an unusual name. Were you named after a state or a tribe?"

"Neither. I was actually named after my great-great-grandmother. She was a member of the Sioux tribe from the North Mississippi Valley."

"You are part Indian? With blonde hair and green eyes?" Yemaya asked, intrigued by the thought.

"Not a drop," Dakota laughed. "I said she was a member of the tribe, not an Indian."

"Ah, a captive then."

"Nope, she wasn't a captive either. She sat on the tribal council for several years, a full-fledged member."

"Okay, I give up. Not a captive, not an Indian. Who was great-great-grandma Dakota?"

"Well, you could say she was an adventurer. From what I've heard and read, she didn't want to settle down on some homestead plowing fields and rearing a dozen kids, so she stole a horse from her stepdad's farm and hightailed it for the hills.

"She pretended to be a man for several years. Apparently, the trappers didn't question her sex. Guess they just assumed she was a he. After all, what kind of woman would want to live a life like theirs—sleeping under the stars, never knowing where the next meal was coming from, or who was behind the next tree to ambush them to steal their furs, food, or dry goods or worse yet, kill them? They thought their way of life was too hard for a woman." Dakota rolled her eyes.

She was about to continue when Yemaya grimaced. Looking down at the blood-soaked bandage around the other woman's leg, she cursed her thoughtlessness.

"Damn. I'm so sorry. I forgot you were hurt. Let's get you taken care of and we'll talk later, okay?"

Nodding, Yemaya limped toward the desk. She felt a warm hand cup her left elbow and smiled slightly.

"It looks worse than it is," she responded, trying to reassure the young woman.

"Sure it does. That's always the case, isn't it?" Dakota snickered, motioning to the night nurse to take control of the injured woman.

"Anyway, you go with nurse...Betty? Nurse Betty, here. I'll wait in the lobby if you still want to hear about Grandma Dakota," she offered.

"Count on it. Stay here. I should be back in a few."

"See you soon."

Yemaya limped into an examination room, and Dakota sat down and took out her notebook. The image of the man with the camera still bothered her. She sketched as close a likeness of him as she could along with a physical description. Fifteen minutes later, she put everything away. The next day, she would go over her notes and enter any details she had forgotten. Leaning her head back against the wall, she closed her eyes and thought about Yemaya.

"So," Yemaya said, "getting back to great-great-grandma Dakota...exactly what did she do to get on the tribal council?"

Dakota put down the cup of tea, her gaze fixated on its contents. Once Yemaya's leg was stitched, she had offered to buy Dakota a drink in return for the details of her distant relative. Yemaya was intrigued by the information she had already learned.

"Um...well...let's see...according to my grandmother, her grandmother was a looney," she answered, stirring the tea.

"Looney?"

"Yeah, looney. Grandma used to say Dakota was 'tetched in the head' because she ran around buck naked through the woods, calling and singing to spirits. She'd chant in strange tongues while dancing around the trees, waving her arms and hands in the air, spinning and twirling like a top. I bet she was a sight to see," Dakota chuckled, gesturing wildly with her arms in an effort to imitate her grandmother.

"I can imagine," Yemaya laughed, visualizing a woman similar to Dakota communing with nature. "Or at least I think I can. So she was crazy...how did that get her a council seat?"

"Grandma said Dakota spent a lot of time in the hills with the mountain people. Like I said, she lived off the land, hunted, skinned animals, fished—those sorts of things. You know, all that woodsy type stuff. Grandma thinks maybe Dakota ate something or smoked something that affected her sensibilities. Most likely, it was the stuff she smoked.

"There was a picture of her sitting on a horse with a cob pipe in her mouth. I bet she found her own brand of weed back then," Dakota joked, looking up from her cup, eyes twinkling. "Anyway, my great-grandmother left a diary describing Dakota's escapades. Seems she was having one of her 'fits,' as great-grams would say, when she came across a young buck treed by a grizzly."

"Buck?" Yemaya interrupted.

"Indian. Anyway, seeing this naked Indian trying to scramble up a 'scrawny sapplin', the sun shining off his firm brown bare Injun butt'—her words, not mine—great-great-grandma starts to 'whoopin' and hollerin' like you wouldn't believe.' Took off her buckskin shirt and began waving it over her head in a circle. Startled the brave so badly, he fell out of the tree onto the bear, which in turn startled the bear enough that it backed up a few feet, confused at the unexpected attacks.

"Next thing you know, great-great-grams is beating this bear with her leather top, screaming and yelling like some crazy person. The bear swiped at her a few times, then, according to the diary, finally got tired of all the racket and being beat on so it took off into the woods."

"I can imagine." Yemaya said, smiling faintly.

"Me too! When the Indian came to his senses, he saw her doing some crazy dance all the while chanting loudly and waving her hands in the air. Great-grams claimed the Indian was more 'skeered' of Dakota than he was of the bear. Thought she was possessed by spirits. He jumped up, hightailed it toward the woods, and tripped and fell, dislocating his shoulder. Great-great-grams grabbed his arm, gave a whoop and yanked it, causing it to slip back in the socket. Turns out he was the son of a Sioux chieftain. He thought she was inhabited with spirits or something because he convinced her to follow him back to the tribe. She lived with the Sioux for several years afterward."

"Phew...quite a story. So, saving the son of a chief made her eligible for a tribal seat?"

"Nah! Indian braves aren't that easy. They showed her plenty of respect for her bravery, but to them, she was just another squaw, albeit somewhat unusual. Crazier than the rest but still just a woman. What got her the seat on the tribal council was her whipping a few bare asses. Apparently, the chief and the elders didn't want the other tribes hearing that a female was able to beat their bravest warriors."

"Especially in those days," Yemaya added.

"Yeah. Grandma said Dakota humiliated several of the braves during the hunts. She'd come back with more game, then tease the young men about being softies or lazy or inept. Used to tell them old squaws could do a better job of providing for the tribe than them. They'd get fired up afterward from drinking, and next thing you know, fights broke out and off came Dakota's top. She'd pounce on some poor unsuspecting victim and swat at him with her shirt, yelling and chanting to the spirits. The men were terrified of her, said she had spirits dancing in her head. The few times someone tried to fight back, she'd do a few flips or kicks, and some brave found himself flat on the ground with great-great-grandma sitting on his chest with a knife pressed against his throat.

"The braves began calling her Maopa, or mosquito creek woman, because they claimed she was like a mosquito— small and annoying but very brave. So to save face, they gave her the status of council member. That way, there was no disgrace in being beaten during the hunts since she was protected by spirits. It was also their way of explaining away how she 'whooped up on so many bare arses.'"

"Sounds like your namesake was quite a woman. How did you come into the picture?" Yemaya asked, leaning forward, her head propped on the palm of her left hand.

"Me? Oh, you mean how'd great-great-grandma get pregnant? Well, she met a French-Canadian trapper. Seems she decided it was about time she reared some kids of her own. She told great-grams she'd always wanted to raise her own tribe of girls just to give 'them thar menfolk something to thank about.' She liked this 'Frenchie's' looks and decided he was a 'fine feddle of a man—good lookin', good breedin stock'—and wanted his baby, not him, mind you, only his baby.

"She seduced him, bedded him, got pregnant, then sent him on his way. Called him a no good, smelly polecat. Told him she'd have the whole Sioux nation after his scalp if he didn't leave the territory pronto. And to prove it, she talked a few bucks into kidnapping him, tying him up, and pouring skunk urine all over him. Then they put him on his horse backward and sent him on his way. Needless to say, Jean-Pierre Lambroux left for lands unknown, never to be seen again. Great-grandma Chayton arrived eight months later."

"Chayton?"

"Yeah, Chayton. It means falcon."

"Interesting...any other Indian names in your family?"

"Several, actually. Mom's name is Teetonka, which means talks too much." Dakota grinned. "And does she ever. If you ever meet her, be prepared to do a *lot* of listening. Everyone calls her Tee for short. Then grandma's name is Naypashni, which stands for strong or courageous. We call her Pashna for short. Grandma had her own escapades, so her name is appropriate enough. I have two cousins, Anchapa and Choumani. I think that's about it for the Indian names."

"Any native blood running around in your veins?"

"Not really...unless Lambroux had some. Dakota stayed with the Sioux for several years, then headed farther west with Chayton. She ended up in Colorado. According to Chayton's diary, her mother died in her forties from an epidemic of some kind that killed a bunch of people. I figured it was dysentery or cholera. Chayton was grown by then. She came back east and settled in Illinois, married a local boy, and had three kids. The rest is history as they say."

"A colorful history for sure," Yemaya said.

"So you listened to me ramble on. How about giving up some of the dark sordid details of your life?" Dakota teased.

"Nothing to give up," Yemaya replied calmly. "Both of my parents died when I was young. As for my history...well, I would describe it as complicated. Speaking of which, I need to get a move on it. I have a lot of things to take care of today, not to mention getting out of these awful clothes and taking a nice hot shower."

"Oh, I get it. You wangled my family history out of me and now you're off and about, eh?" Dakota chided. "No fair, you know."

Yemaya stood and stretched. "No one ever said it was, and I never *wangle*. Tell you what, though. You call me later this week, and I will tell you a little about myself. Maybe even give you something you can write in that notepad of yours to make your boss happy," she added, walking toward the exit. "See you!" she called as she walked out the hospital door.

Well, I'll be damned, Dakota thought. *An actual interview.*

Paying the bill, she headed for her car. Climbing into the driver's seat, she started the engine. Suddenly, it dawned on her something wasn't quite right.

"Son of a bitch!" Dakota exclaimed, slapping the steering wheel. "She never gave me her number and didn't even ask for mine."

Irritated at herself for having been tricked so easily, she slammed the car into gear, floored the accelerator, and spun the wheels as she headed down the highway. What had been one of the most interesting nights of her life had just turned to worms, and Dakota was not happy.

Chapter Three

Yemaya unbuttoned her silk blouse and tossed it on the bed. Blue leather slacks quickly followed along with black silk underwear. Walking to the bathroom, she turned on the shower and adjusted the temperature.

Just as she was about to step in, she remembered the doctor had warned her about getting her wound wet. With a sigh, she turned the shower off. The shark bite would heal within a few days. She always healed quickly. For tonight, though, a hot bath would feel better.

Moments later, lying in the oversized whirlpool, her right leg draped over the edge, she leaned back, closed her eyes, and replayed the evening's events. Everything had gone well until Suzanne had discovered the crack in the platform. Crack wasn't exactly accurate. It was more like a hairline cut over two meters long.

By itself, it would have little impact on the stability of the platform. It was the depth and shape of the cut that concerned her. More than two-thirds of the thickness of the glass had been compromised by a fairly straight line running along the width of the platform. The weight of the platform, along with the two attendants was enough to create a break. Add her weight to it, a little vibration, which was inevitable considering the volume of water being moved by the great white, and the results were a foregone conclusion.

The performance had been sabotaged. The question was why. Did someone want to scare her attendants or were they after bigger fish—namely her? Was a scare the end result of their attempts or was it murder? More important, why hadn't she sensed the shark's attack? Never before had Shezara gotten through her defenses. She would have to rethink the events once she had slept. In the meantime, she'd call her lawyer Sonny Marino and her brother Raidon later in the day. They would investigate it further.

Putting that aside, she thought about Dakota. Considering how horribly wrong the evening had begun, the hours spent with the young woman had been quite pleasurable. Yemaya was intrigued not only by the woman's history, but also by the woman herself.

No one could argue she wasn't attractive with her sparkling green eyes and blonde hair cut into a short pixie with bangs ending just above the eyebrows that framed an oval face. At approximately 5'6", Dakota had the compact body of an athlete. It was obvious she was either active in sports or spent a lot of time in the gym.Yemaya enjoyed the stories about her grandmother, but it was the other woman's voice she had been drawn to. The faint Midwestern accent complemented her soft-spoken words.

Warm water and bubbles swirled soothingly around Yemaya, and tired muscles relaxed under the gentle massage of the jets. Within minutes, her thoughts slipped gently away, giving her exhausted mind a reprieve from the day's events.

Yemaya's nose twitched slightly as her brain analyzed the faint odor penetrating her slumber—wild flowers. Wrinkling her brow, she concentrated in an effort to open her eyes. How did wild flowers get into the bathroom? Slowly, she opened one eyelid and looked around. A meadow surrounded by huge oak trees encompassed her view. Brilliant flowers of every color painted the meadow. Small monarch butterflies floated from one blossom to another, tasting the delicate pollens. The sound of running water, mixed with the chattering of squirrels created an idyllic scene.

Quickly, she straightened up. She was lying on soft green grass, the back of her head resting on the palms of her cupped hands. Deep within the forest, wild birds argued noisily to establish territories or fend off unwanted attention. It was too idyllic to be real, until her ears were assailed by the high-pitched screech of a wild animal. Pale eyes turned, searching for whatever had made such an awful sound.

Within seconds, a half-naked woman charged from the darkened forest into the light, swinging something in her hand. The screeching became a melodic chant as the figure twirled, jumped and ran, arms swaying back and forth above her head, her face turned upward toward the sky.

As if sensing Yemaya's presence, she stopped her wild dance to stare curiously at the stranger sitting in the middle of the meadow. After watching her for a few minutes, she waved excitedly and walked over to Yemaya, plopping down next to her. Plucking a purple flower, she leaned forward, offering it to the startled woman.

"So it's 'bout time ya decided to come callin'," the wild-looking woman announced, her breasts swaying slightly when she leaned backward, her arms bracing her in an upright sitting position.

Yemaya couldn't help but stare at the nicely rounded orbs. The dark nipples stood erect. The breasts were small and golden. Blinking, she shifted her gaze to the green eyes staring at her good-naturedly.

"Come calling? This is a dream. I never knew you existed until Dakota told me about you this evening. You are just a product of a very tired brain," she replied, resisting the temptation to lower her gaze.

The other woman smiled, revealing straight white teeth. Her cheeks creased on each side, displaying two dimples.

"That so?" she asked, her accent heavy with sarcasm. "Well, ifn that's what ya think, how come you're eyeing my teets like they was somethin' to be plucked from a tree and et?"

Yemaya blushed, a rare event. *Do people blush in dreams?* she thought.

"Well, you *are* topless, you know. I am not used to seeing women running around half-naked like some wood nymph, especially in my dreams."

"Nymph? Ah, ya mean the fairy folk. Woods here is filled with fairy folk. We calls 'em spirits, though. They talks ta me and I talks back. I kin tell ya who and what is traipsin' through them trees day or night, and ya seen a fair share of nekkid teets now. I knowed ya has a special likin' for the ladies. We's alike that way, ya knows, so don't go trying to fool this old woman," she chided, slapping Yemaya's right knee. "But where's my mannahs? The name's Dakota, but ya already knowed that, didn't ya?" she stated. "Just likes ya knows a lot of thangs," she added, nodding sagely.

"I guess I did, and what do you mean I know lots of things?"

"Well, now. I don't need to go tellin' ya what ya knows and what ya don't. Right now I be thinkin' ya thinks I taint real."

"I take it you consider yourself real and not some figment of my imagination?"

"Figment? That a fancy way a saying ya made me up? Like thinkin' maybe ya is tetched in the head a wee bit?"

"Yes, that is one way of putting it. Am I making you up? Probably to some extent. I mean, I went to sleep in my jacuzzi...uh...tub, and next thing I know, here I am."

"Well, maybe ya did and maybe ya didn't. How would I knowed ifn I was made up anyways? Ya needs to ask yerself that more'n ya needs to ask me. Then ya needs to ask yerself why would ya go an' do somethin' so peculiar," Dakota suggested.

"Nothing peculiar about having a dream about you. Your great-great-granddaughter told me about you this evening. I found the stories interesting, so I guess my mind is just processing everything I heard."

"Well, then. Guess maybe ya figures ya has the answer. Far bes it from me to be settin' ya on the right trail when ya knows what ya knows," Dakota chuckled, green eyes twinkling brightly. "Guess I might as well be movin' on. Got lots of fairy folk to jawbone with, ya knows. Trouble's brewin' in the darkness, and we has to do some figurin' ifn we're gonna win the next scuffle. I'll be a seein' ya sometime soon, magic woman, maybe at the gatherin'. Now ya better get on back to that thar jacoozee thing. Water's growin' cold, taint good to be catchin' a chill even for the likes of you."

Dakota stood and wiped the grass from her deerskin breeches. Walking toward the woods, she turned, smiling gently.

"Don't cha forget to give my respects to that grandchile of mine. She's a good one," she yelled. "Oh and them teets of hers are well worth lookin' at. Ya jest might get lucky if ya plays yer cards right. I dun good with that one," she added, laughing at Yemaya's startled expression. Waving goodbye, she disappeared into the shadows.

Yemaya felt cold. The water had cooled considerably by the time she awoke. Shaking her head, she looked around the bathroom. Nothing seemed out of place.

"What a strange dream. I guess Dakota's story had more of an effect on me than I thought," she sighed, exhausted.

Stepping from the tub, she grabbed an oversized bath towel, dried off before wrapping it around her, and walked into the bedroom. The huge bed with multicolored flannel sheets looked so inviting she didn't bother to slip into her favorite tank top. Instead, she crawled under the sheet, closed her eyes, and fell quickly asleep but not before laughter echoed softly through her weary mind.

"Are you sure about this?" Sonny asked, having listened patiently to his client's description of the events the night before.

"I am sure, Sonny. This was no accident. Someone cut the Plexiglas almost completely through. We were lucky no one was seriously injured or killed," Yemaya replied.

"You have any ideas who would do this? Piss anyone off lately?" he half joked.

"Sonny, I always anger someone, but if you think it might be a competitor, I disagree. The well-known ones have no reason."

"In your mind, maybe. Don't sell yourself short—or them. Everyone is curious about you, and you've developed quite a cult following. But if you don't think it's another illusionist, it has to be someone with a personal vendetta," he surmised.

"Possibly," Yemaya said. "Or interested in me or my family. There have been some unusual inquiries into my government records lately. Raidon was going to check on it for me."

"Well, either way, it's going to be a problem. I'll let him know about this when he contacts me. It's a shame he got called back to the homeland, but it seems someone has been asking a lot of questions about the family. In the meantime, I'll put out feelers and talk to a few contacts to see if any rumors are in the pipeline about you. Try to keep a low profile and stay out of trouble until we see what this is about," Sonny admonished.

"Low profile, eh? I have one more show to do before going home. Not to mention settling things with the sea aquarium and the insurance companies. No way will I be able to do the Charleston show now."

"I'll take care of everything till Raidon returns. You just take care of yourself. Later, kiddo."

"Later, Sonny, and thanks. Just tell Raidon to call me when he gets back."

Hanging up the phone, Yemaya leaned back in her chair and stared out the penthouse window. She had just remembered that she hadn't left her phone number with Dakota the night before or gotten her number. A quick call to the ticketing agency got her nowhere. Apparently, the ticket had been purchased through an organization by someone wishing to remain anonymous.

"Damn. Nothing is going right," Yemaya cursed. Pushing a speed dial number, she waited impatiently for the other party to pick up.

"Hello. Sonny Marino, speaking."

"Sonny, this is Yemaya again. I need you to do me another favor. I met a journalist last night at the hospital. She was also at the performance. I need to get in touch with her, but she bought her ticket through an agency. Can you track her down for me?"

"Personal or business?" Sonny asked.

"Both, actually. She was sitting in the fifth row, seat fourteen. And, Sonny? I would appreciate it if you made this a priority."

"I've never known you to mix business with pleasure. What's so special about this woman?"

"Well, for one, she may have seen something. And two, my reasons are none of your business. Just do it, okay?"

"Sure. No problem. I'll get right on it." It was obvious Sonny's mind was going a mile a minute over the possibilities of why Yemaya was taking a personal interest in a stranger.

"You are wrong on all accounts," she stated. "So put that overactive imagination of yours to sleep."

"Hey, you're always doing that to me. How do you know what I'm thinking?"

"I am a mind reader, Sonny. Surely, you have guessed that by now," she said with a smirk. "In the meantime, thanks. I owe you one."

With Sonny handling the insurance claims and settling with the aquarium, Yemaya decided to check on Suzanne. A phone call would have sufficed, but she felt obligated to pay a personal visit to the young woman to make sure she was getting the proper care. Insurance would cover all the bills, but it didn't ensure good medical treatment.

Yemaya spent the afternoon at the hospital with Suzanne. When she was finally released, arrangements were made to take her home in a limousine and to have a nurse spend the night so the injured woman had some company. By the time things were settled, it was late in the evening, too late to do anything but catch a bite to eat and head home.

Chapter Four

"What do you mean someone may have seen you? It was dark for Christ's sake," the man exclaimed angrily. "And these pictures are trash. Two pictures. I'm paying you $1,500 for two lousy pictures. I pay $500 for the ticket, and this is the best you can do? You can't even see her face. It's all blurry. I thought you said you were a professional photographer," he screamed, throwing the photos on the cluttered mahogany desk before strolling toward the large picture window overlooking the bay.

"Sorry, Mr. Chisholm. Like I said, it was dark, and I don't know why her face is blurry. Everyone else's is clear enough even if it was dark. I can lighten them up for you," he offered.

"I don't care about the others, you asshole. I want a picture of Lysanne," he replied angrily. "I want a $1,500 picture of her...*not* shit like this. Do you understand me?"

"Yes, sir. I'll get one, sir, but it won't be easy."

"I don't want to hear that, Jones. I want results. What's so difficult about taking a quick picture of this woman?"

"They screened everyone for cameras and recorders before entering the main room. I was lucky I found someone I could bribe," the balding little man whined. "It cost me a hundred bucks," he added, wiping his sweating forehead.

"Considering I just paid $1,500 for nothing, I'm sure you don't expect me to pay you back," his boss replied coldly.

"On, no, Mr. Chisholm. Not at all. I was just explaining how I got in and the difficulties. Anyway, everything happened so fast, I couldn't get my camera out in time, then the flash must've attracted the young woman's attention because that's when she looked my way. I'm sure she couldn't see my face. It was very dark."

"We can't take any chances. What did she look like and where was she sitting?" he demanded.

"Uh..I think she was in the fifth or sixth aisle."

Turning quickly, Robert Chisholm strolled toward the nervous man, stopping in front of him.

"What do you mean fifth or sixth aisle, Jones? Which was it?"

"Sixth. It was the sixth, I'm sure," Jones stammered.

"You're sure?"

"Yeah. It was the sixth, and she was in the thirteenth seat," he added, stepping slightly back.

"Then call around and see who was seated there and take care of her. You *do* know what I mean, right, Jones?"

"Sure, Mr. Chisholm. But honestly, I don't think she saw me very well. It was really dark."

"We can't take any chances. Take care of it. And let me know when the job's done. Now leave," the boss ordered.

Eddy Jones scurried from the room, sweat pouring down his cheeks and dripping onto his wrinkled polyester suit. He dreaded the meetings with Robert Chisholm.

"Fucking asshole," he muttered under his breath. "Guy thinks he can treat people like shit because he has money. One of these days..." The words faded when he remembered the rooms leading to Chisholm's office were monitored.

He would make a few calls. It wouldn't be hard to find the woman or to make arrangements to have her taken care of.

Brenda Simpson had just finished discussing Chinese art with her eleventh-grade class. She loved teaching and regretted the thought of retirement at the end of the year.

Still, with trips planned to Southeast Asia, specifically Thailand, Cambodia, and Burma, she felt reborn. The enthusiasm and energy she had directed toward advancing her students' interests in the arts was now being diverted to preparations for an eight-month odyssey in the area of the world she found the most interesting. At fifty-seven and single, she managed to stay in reasonably good shape. Exercising three times a week at the local gym for the past two years had ensured she would be able to make the treks across much of that part of Asia.

Gathering her books, she hurried from the classroom. That afternoon, she needed to catch a flight to Charleston, South Carolina. In less than five hours, she would be at the sea aquarium to watch Yemaya Lysanne, the world-class illusionist who had recently been dominating entertainment magazines.

Thanks to the raffle she had won two months earlier at the annual parent/student/teacher picnic, she had an opportunity to witness a once-in-a-lifetime event. Reaching into her pants pocket, she pulled out the shiny silver and blue admittance ticket.

"Admit one," she read aloud with a smile. "And I'm that one. Guess Lady Luck was with me that day."

"You talking to yourself again, Brenda?"

Looking up, she saw Bill Langley staring at her, barely successful at hiding his infamous quirky smile.

"As usual, Bill," she replied, winking. "I have to catch my flight in time for the show."

"Show? Oh, yeah, the lady magician," he teased.

"Not a magician, an illusionist, one of the best I hear."

"Yeah, so I hear. You wouldn't have a spare ticket, would you?" he half joked.

"I wouldn't even have this one at $500 a shot if I hadn't bought that raffle ticket a couple of months ago. One of the luckiest days of my life," she commented, showing him the ticket.

Bill quickly glanced at the ticket in Brenda's hand.

"Good seating. You'll get a great view from there. Well, take some pictures for me if you can, okay?"

Not wanting to disappoint her teaching associate, Brenda just nodded. Later she could tell him cameras weren't allowed.

"Gotta run, Bill. I'll see you Monday."

"Sure thing, Brenda. Then you can tell me if she's as good as the papers say. Have a great time."

Brenda barely made it through the scanner and to her seat before the lights dimmed. The stage in front of the aquarium filled with a smoky mist. A shadowy figure walked through the swirling smoke and emerged in front of the audience. From that moment, the events of the evening would forever stay transfixed in her mind. By the time everything was over, she felt exhausted from the emotional stress. She would definitely have something to tell Bill and the other teachers on Monday.

The weekend passed quickly. Preparations for her overseas trip were finalized. Only four more weeks and she would be on her way. In the meantime, she knew her associates would be waiting for her in the conference room. The event at the sea aquarium had taken up most of the Saturday morning headlines. Even her mother had called to hear all about it. It took over two hours to answer her questions.

Brenda juggled her briefcase, purse, and stack of paperwork as she locked the door to her car. Turning, she looked in both directions before crossing the road and headed into the subway system of Atlanta. It was a twenty-minute ride to her stop and another ten-minute walk to the high school in Doraville. With luck, she wouldn't have to wait very long for the train.

At six thirty in the morning, the subways were crowded with commuters. MARTA was one of the most efficient public transport systems in the world. Rarely were there delays, and that morning was no different. As Brenda stepped up to the edge of the platform, she could hear the roar of the train coming through the tunnel. A strong breeze preceded the appearance of a light in the distance. Glancing toward the oncoming train, she sighed, relieved at the prospect of settling into one of the seats to preview some of the paperwork in her arms. Just as the train was exiting the tunnel, she felt a body press against her, forcing her closer to the edge of the platform. Pushing backward, she turned to say something to the offender and lost her balance.

Dakota spent the weekend writing a brief report to send to her boss. After phoning him about the events on Friday night, he was more than willing to sponsor one ticket on her behalf. His only request was a summary of everything she had managed to gather so far. The ticket for her flight to Montreal had been emailed to her and the show ticket overnighted.

"I hate early morning flights," Dakota grumbled as she sat looking out the window. Planes were taxiing in and out, but Gate A-6 was quiet since her layover was more than three hours. A young couple with a sleeping baby was in the corner whispering softly, looking as if they needed a good night's sleep. An older woman was reading a popular lesbian novel but was trying to conceal the title with her left hand. Dakota chuckled. She had read the book several times. It was one of her favorite traveling books.

Distracted by an elderly gentleman accompanied by two younger men dressed in business suits, she caught just a few words of the conversation.

"Yeah, another one killed on MARTA. How many has it been this year?"

Dakota didn't hear the reply, but being a journalist, she was now curious.

"Well, you'd think they'd put up some rails to make people stay back some, wouldn't you?" the young man responded.

Getting up, Dakota decided to purchase a local paper. Quickly scanning the front page, she found the article about an accident on MARTA.

"Woman dies in subway accident." *A local school teacher was killed when she fell in front of a MARTA train Monday morning. Witnesses say it appears she may have been accidentally pushed when a white male turned suddenly to speak to someone behind him. Police have identified the deceased as Brenda Simpson, 57. The identity of the man has not been determined. Eyewitnesses describe him as approximately 5-foot-7 with a slender build, thinning brown hair, and wearing a dark suit and glasses. They have requested he contact them. No charges are pending.*

Simpson was a teacher at the high school in Doraville. Her friends and colleagues have described her as a warm caring teacher who will be sorely missed.

"Brenda was an exceptional human being. She loved her students and her colleagues," said William Langley, a fellow teacher. "She was such an interesting person. Everyone was looking forward to her return to work today because she had just gotten back from watching a magic show in Charleston. We'll miss her."

Wow, that's freaky," Dakota thought. *She was at the same show as me. I wonder if I talked with her.*

Flipping to the next page, she began reading about the city's attempt to close one of the local private nightclubs. The article was sketchy, but the gist of the report was the club was a popular dancing and rendezvous spot for the gay community, although many straight people frequented it also. It seemed the mayor and council members had created some new zoning ordinances that changed the status of the nightclub from private to public. Dakota finished reading the story and threw the paper on the seat next to her in disgust.

"When is all this crap gonna stop?" she muttered. "Why can't people just mind their own business?"

Leaning back against the wall, she closed her eyes and dozed until her flight number for Montreal was called.

It took Eddy only four hours to track the owner of the ticket to aisle six, seat thirteen. Offer enough money to people, and it was amazing how quickly information could be gotten. What simplified it even more was the person had won the ticket at a raffle during a school function, so getting her personal information was easy. By Sunday afternoon, he had located Brenda Simpson's home address and school. Sunday night, he had taken three photos, checked out her habits with a couple of neighbors, and knew exactly what time she left for work.

Neighbors were eager to talk about her, especially when he identified himself as an investigator doing a background check on the teacher because she had been nominated for Best Teacher of the Year award for Georgia. Obviously, he needed to check into her personal life to make sure she was worthy of such a prestigious recognition.

All that was left was for him to wait at the MARTA station nearest her. Early in the morning, it was easy to spot the car the neighbors described. He had no doubt he would recognize her once she entered the subway, so he had gone ahead and positioned himself against the wall.

As he watched the blonde woman walk past him, he turned his head nonchalantly to look at the MARTA map. Slowly pushing away from the wall, he followed her toward the edge of the platform, positioning himself behind her. He began fumbling in his pockets as if looking for something. As the train cleared the tunnel, he pretended to be bumped and in return bumped the woman. He looked behind him, appearing irritated, then turned quickly back and fell forward just as the woman turned to look at him.

For a split second, his eyes met her surprised look, then she fell backward onto the rails in front of the train. Eddy instinctively grabbed for her to keep her from falling, but the crowd had shuffled slightly, causing him to miss. Then the screams of horrified commuters and the pushing and shoving to get away or to get a better look made it impossible for him to see anything. Not that there was much to see. The train covered whatever remains there were of the woman. Turning away, he elbowed his way through the crowd and ran up the stairs. Once on the outside, he bent over, gasping raggedly for air, bile heaving up from his gut. It took all his energy to control the urge to vomit.

"Fuck, fuck, fuck," he groaned. "What a fuckup. It wasn't her, it wasn't her," he kept repeating. "He's gonna fuckin' kill me if he finds out."

Hurrying to his parked car, he opened the door, slipped inside, and put his forehead against the steering wheel.

"I gotta think of something," he mumbled.

Robert Chisholm stood staring out the picture window at the ocean, no longer impressed by the waves slapping at the golden sandy beach. He had looked at it since he was seven years old and had known even then this would all be his.

Charles Wentworth III inherited his wealth, but it didn't stop him from working hard to attain the position of CEO in his family's business. He had learned the basics of each phase of publishing to understand what the company employees did to make the business successful, and for that, he was highly respected by them and management.

His rise to power was quick, but few would accuse his father of nepotism when he finally made Charles the president of Wentworth Publications. At thirty-two, he eventually married the daughter of his father's best friend, more as a convenience than out of love. Christine had been a good wife and companion. Seven years into the marriage, she died of breast cancer.

Childless, Charles spent the next twelve years running the business. It wasn't until he met Cynthia Chisholm that he took an interest in life again. She was eighteen years his junior, tall, slender, redheaded, energetic, and an employee of his company. His senior vice president hired her as his personal secretary. Charles pulled rank and acquired her for himself. Soon they were having dinners together and frequenting the local nightclubs. The fact that she had a five-year-old son didn't deter Charles in his attempts at wooing the young woman. Eventually, they married, and Charles willingly adopted her son, Robert.

During the next several years, Charles did his best to bond with the boy. To most people, it appeared he was successful. Charles, however, knew better. Robert was always respectful to him when others were present, but Charles was astute enough to recognize the hatred in the eyes behind the smiling face.

He understood the child's resentment over having to share Cynthia with another man and hoped it would pass. It never did. Cynthia was a doting mom, wanting to give her son every benefit money could offer. She was truly fond of Charles, although she never really loved him. Still Charles could not have asked for a better wife. The fact she couldn't have more children saddened him but had also made him more determined to groom Robert to take over the family business. This seemed to please Cynthia and Robert.

At twenty-eight, Robert felt he was ready to take over Wentworth Publications. His stepfather was in his mid-seventies. Robert thought he should have retired a long time before, but Charles was in excellent health. Nothing short of an accident would give Robert his rightful place.

On his twenty-ninth birthday, Robert got his wish. Cynthia and his Charles were on their way to his penthouse in Miami Beach when they were struck by a taxicab. The driver said he was distracted by an object thrown at his front window. Cursing, he turned to yell at some young hoodlums and didn't see the older couple step onto the crosswalk.

Both died from the impact, leaving Robert alone and sole heir of his stepfather's business. No one was charged, and Robert didn't pursue legal action against the driver. Shrugging philosophically, he had merely commented that "an accident was an accident."

Those who were aware of his ambitious nature found his response interesting, if not downright suspicious. Rumors circulated about the "accident," but since there weren't any witnesses to say otherwise, they faded quickly.

Robert Chisholm Wentworth became the CEO of Wentworth Publications. Shortly after assuming the position, he dropped his adopted name, claiming he wanted to be known for his own accomplishments, not those of his stepfather. He had approached the board members about changing the name of the company but met with so much hostility that he backed down, apologizing by explaining he was just trying to give the company a new image. No one bought the explanation, but an uneasy truce was called.

Time passed and Robert Chisholm proved to be an astute businessman. The company expanded into other lines of business. The entertainment field was of special interest to him. While reviewing a few publications of *Magical Illusions*, one of his company's newly acquired magazines, he noticed an article about Yemaya Lysanne, along with a small picture of her in costume. From then on, he tracked her rise to fame.

He attended a few of her performances, studying her illusions, trying to unravel the mysteries behind them and her. Unable to do either and not willing to accept failure, he was determined to solve the mysteries surrounding her.

His instincts told him there was more to the woman than illusions. No one could explain her disappearing tricks. Her background was a mystery. The few bits of information uncovered indicated that she had arrived in the U.S. at age twenty-one. Her passport identified her as a citizen of Moldova, supposedly from the town of Taraclia.

Curious to know more about her, Chisholm sent two investigators to the town three years before. After receiving a report of their arrival and that they had picked up a few leads, they were never heard from again. A second pair was sent six months later. They too disappeared.

When he tried to hire locals, he was advised to drop his investigation, and no amount of money could persuade them otherwise. All channels to the country had been closed to him. Frustrated and unused to being thwarted, he called his government sources, only to be told there was nothing they could do. Chisholm did not like feeling impotent and vowed he would discover the reason for her anonymity and secrecy.

A knock on the door interrupted his thoughts.

"Enter!" he ordered, turning as his secretary stepped through the opening.

"Mr. Chisholm, Mr. Jones asks for a moment of your time."

"Send him in, Ms. Randall, and no calls."

"Yes, sir."

Eddy Jones stepped cautiously into the room, sweat dripping from his brow.

"For Christ's sake, Jones. Quit dripping on the carpet," Chisholm hissed.

"Um...oh....sorry, Mr. Chisholm," he apologized, wiping his face with his sleeve.

"Well, what is it?"

"It's-it's all taken care of, Mr. Chisholm," Jones stuttered.

"Permanently?"

"Yes, sir, permanently. The...um...customer had an unfortunate accident in Atlanta. She lost her balance and fell in front of an oncoming train in the subway."

"Any witnesses?"

"Well, yes, sir. She lost her balance and fell. Very unfortunate."

"And what do the police have to say about this unfortunate incident?"

"They ruled it an accident. There won't be any problems," Eddy added, relieved his employer accepted his story.

"Good job."

Walking to his desk, he opened a drawer and pulled out a large brown envelope. Throwing it on the desk, he turned toward Jones.

"This is a plane ticket to Montreal. Reservations for your motel are at the Lord Berry. I want you at her next performance. Your ticket is also there, along with $2,000. It's a complimentary one for the charitable contribution I made to Miami Children's Hospital. It cost me eight grand, so don't go losing it. That'll be more than enough with the exchange rate."

"Sure, boss. You want me to try and take more pictures?"

"Hell, no. Someone saw you the last time and look what happened. Who knows who else might've seen you? Besides, I don't want some smart reporter connecting two deaths with Lysanne's shows."

"It's another country, boss. Who could do that?"

Robert Chisholm glared at Eddy.

"Damn it, Jones! Are you always so fucking stupid? We're talking Canada, not some godforsaken place like Russia. Reporters follow people like her all the time. Just keep an eye on her and try to get something worth the money I'm paying you. You think you can do that?"

"Sure, boss. No problem."

"Good, now get out. I've got work to do," Chisholm snapped.

Chapter Five

Dakota threw her luggage on the chair. Falling backward on the bed, she sighed. The flight had been smooth, but the layover in Atlanta was a bitch. A warm bath and a nap was called for, but first she needed to check at the front desk to see if the overnight package arrived. Dialing 0, she waited for someone to pick up.

"Bon après-midi, reception. Comment puis-je vous aider?"

"Oh, hi. I mean, bonjour. This is room 223. I'm expecting a package this afternoon. Has it arrived yet?"

"Un moment, mademoiselle. I weel check for you, yes?"

"Thank you."

After a few minutes, the clerk was back on the phone.

"Allo? Mademoiselle?"

"Yes."

"Ze package has not arrived. I weel let you know when it does, yes?"

"Yes, please. Would you please have the front desk ring my room in about two hours?"

"Oui, mademoiselle. Ef you need anything, you will call me? I am Nathalie."

"Thank you, Nathalie. Have a good evening."

"Vous aussi. Au revoir, mademoiselle."

Dakota didn't spend much time soaking. Getting caught up on her sleep was the bigger priority. Crawling under the sheets, she closed her eyes and drifted off.

The sounds of chanting woke her. Opening her eyes, she was confused by flames dancing in front of her. Blinking, she looked down and noticed she was wearing deerskin breeches and top.

"What the—?"

"Breeches."

"Breeches?" Dakota asked, looking across the campfire at an older version of herself.

"Breeches. Theys be breeches. Ya knows...deerskin leggins."

Looking back down, she gasped.

"But...but...they only cover my legs. The...um...rest of me is visible."

"Of course ya is. What good is havin' that thar bush of yourn covered up? Why ifn ya gets a call from nature ya'd have ta takes them down in a hurry. Worse yet, how would ya go cleaning yerself up? This way, ya just has to let the breeze blow through ifn ya pisses. Course, ifn ya has to do the other, grass is for that," she smirked.

Dakota shuddered at the thought of using grass or any plant, for that matter. What if she chose the wrong thing? She had heard stories of people who had camped and grabbed poison ivy. They actually had to be hospitalized for several days. The itching had been unbearable.

"I don't think I need to think about this at the moment. I can't believe I'm even having this conversation."

"Wahl, then. What might be on yer mind that ya needs to jawbone with me now? Ya never has before."

"Me? I just laid lay down to take a nap. I wasn't even thinking of you."

"Ya twern't? Seems ta me ya was a talkin' 'bout me a few days back. Seems ta me ya had lots of thangs to tell that magic woman," the older woman said.

"You mean Yemaya? How do you know about her? This is some type of weird dream, isn't it? I was telling her about you, and now I'm having strange dreams."

"Seems y'all has this here feexashun on dreamin'. The magic woman knowed everything and now ya claims to knowed it all."

"What do you mean Yemaya knowed...knows...knew everything? Only reason you know about her is because we talked about you. You can't know more than I do."

"There ya goes tellin' me what I ken't be knowin'. Well, youngun. I knowed she's a pawerful magic woman. And I knowed the two of ya were meant to meet up. *And* I knowed the two of yas is headin' for some big trouble. Darkness is comin' a callin', and it's gonna take a heap of magic and help from the spirits if yas gonna live through it."

"What kind of darkness, Granny? What do you see?"

"Ken't tell, youngun. I just feels it in my bones and the spirits be restless. They be whisperin' about the darkness, and ya seems to be somehow connected to it."

"Darkness. What darkness?"

"Not sure, chile. But when da spirits start a twitterin' like they bes, it ken't be good. Ya gots to be real careful now cuz there's somethin' a brewin'. That's all I knowed, except the magic woman is gonna need yer help, and yer gonna need hers. Ya bes pardners now."

"Granny, I don't even know her. I met her once. I can't even get in touch with her now unless I can attract her attention at her next performance."

Grandma Dakota slapped her hands against her legs, laughing hard.

"Why, chile, ya already has that. More'n ya thinks. For sure, that one noticed ya. She sees a lot of things, she does. Mind ya, she's a bit tall with a bit of darkness to her, but she's good. Yesseree. If I wasn't daid, I'd be beddin' her right now, snugglin' up all close and warm, runnin' my fingers through that thar long dark hair. She gots some mighty fine teets if ya knowed what I mean. Bet she could even make the likes of me scream like a banshee," she chuckled.

Shocked, Dakota's jaw dropped.

"Granny!"

"Oh, dun ya be a grannyin' me like some innocent. Ya ken't wait to give that one a roll in the hay, so don't be getting' all high and mighty, missy. Ya liked the gals all yer life and ya knowed it. An ya don't knowed a thing 'bout screamin'. I seed ya. Ya thinks that little tingle is all they is. Well, I's here to tell ya, one night with the magic woman and ya'd be a lappin' at that thar bush like a dog lappin' gravy. Ya takes after me that way." Grandma Dakota grinned.

Blushing, Dakota glanced down, then quickly raised her eyes after glimpsing her pubic hairs. This had to be a dream, a warped one, too. Who in their right mind would dress up like this, even in a dream, let alone be discussing this type of thing with her grandmother?

"Well, now, missy, theys just happens ta be what I wore for years. Those breeches are warm in winter and likes I says before...cunvenyent."

"How can they be warm? I'd freeze my butt, and my snatc...um...the rest of me in this thing."

"Hee..hee...hee...That's why ya needs a pardner. She'd take care of warmin' that thar bush of yourn. But enough jawin'. Ya needs to get back to wheres ya at. That thar package is come."

"But—"

The ringing of a phone aroused Dakota from her dream.

"Hello."

"Bon nuit, mademoiselle. You wished to be awakened, yes?"

"Yes, I did. Thank you, Nathalie. Has my package arrived?"

"Oui, it is at the front desk. Do you wish it to be brought to your room?"

"That would be great, thanks."

"Very good. Au revoir, mademoiselle."

"Goodbye."

A few minutes later, the package containing her ticket to Yemaya's next performance was delivered to her room. While she was waiting, she thought about the strange dream. It definitely was not anything like she had ever experienced before. Her imagination must have really been affected by the conversation about her grandmother.

"If that's what granny was like, she was one strange woman," Dakota mumbled as she prepared to go out for dinner.

The Hotel Bonaventure's manager greeted Yemaya enthusiastically.

"Bonjour, Mademoiselle Lysanne. Comment ça va?"

"Très bien, Monsier Duval. Merci. Et vous?"

"Bien aussi. Puis-je vous montrer votre suite?" he asked tentatively.

"D'accord."

"Nous avons tout arrangé selon vos spécifications. Vous êtes enregistrée sous le nom de Jennifer Sommers. Le personnel a été avisé de l'importance de garder votre identité secrète; vous pouvez compter sur leur loyauté et leur discrétion?

"Encore une fois, merci, Monsieur Duval."

After the formality of inspecting the penthouse, Yemaya walked onto the terrace overlooking the vast garden. Ducks swam in the small landscaped ponds. She was always impressed by the atmosphere and service at this particular hotel, not to mention the staff's ability to keep her identity secret.

Returning to the bedroom and her luggage, she unlocked the suitcases. A ringing phone interrupted the unpacking.

"Bonsoir, Mademoiselle Sommers. Vous avez un appel de votre frère."

"Merci. Hello, brother. How was your trip?"

"It went well, but there is trouble brewing. Someone is trying to acquire a lot of information about you, and apparently, that person is very powerful."

"Did Sonny tell you about my last performance?"

"Yes. Do you have any idea who might have sabotaged the platform?"

"I am sure it is not any of my fellow illusionists. It would not benefit them. I think it might have something to do with this person who has been trying to get information from my contacts in the U.S. government. Of course, they do not know much, so that is of no consequence. I am more concerned about one of my people getting hurt or killed."

"Do you wish me to send our security?" Raidon asked.

"No, that would only let them know I suspect something. I can handle things from this end. After the Montreal show, I will be heading home. We can discuss this further when I get there."

"Very well, sister. Be careful. Until we find out who is behind these attempts, we must be vigilant."

"I will, Raidon. And you, too. This may have to do with more than just me. Our people cannot afford to be exposed to public scrutiny. I will be home by the end of the week. Until then."

"Be safe."

Yemaya had just settled in bed when the phone rang again.

"Bonsoir."

"Bonsoir, Mademoiselle Sommers. Vous avez un appel de Monsieur Marino."

"Merci. Hello, Sonny."

"Good evening, Yemaya. Good news. I found the whereabouts of your journalist, a Ms. Dakota Devereaux, to be exact."

"Where can I reach her?"

"Well, right about now, I imagine she's in bed at the Best Western Europa. Room 223."

"You mean she is here in Montreal?" Yemaya asked, stunned by the knowledge.

"That's exactly what I mean. Apparently, this young woman has a fixation with you. She's attended several of your shows lately. As to the other matters, I still don't have any leads about the sabotage, but I've got people investigating a few angles. When will you be heading home?"

"The end of the week at the latest. Please handle anything that comes up in the States. I should be back in a few months."

"No problem. I'll contact you if anything unusual crops up. Enjoy your stay and give my regards to the family."

"Thank you, Sonny. I appreciate your efforts. Bye."

Hanging up the phone, Yemaya decided to send a message to Dakota. Dialing the front desk, she recognized the receptionist's voice.

"Bon nuit, Michelle. Veuillez livrer une note à Mademoiselle Devereaux, à l'hôtel Best Western Europa, chambre 223, s'il-vous-plaît." She then dictated a short message.

Dakota was just walking into her room when the phone rang.

"Hello."

"Ms. Devereaux, I have a message for you from a Ms. Sommers."

"Ms. Sommers? I don't know anyone by that name. What does the message say?"

"She says, 'I would like to meet with you for breakfast to further discuss your great-great-grandmother Dakota. If possible, please join me at the Hotel Bonaventura at eight a.m.' It's signed Jennifer Sommers. Do you want me to reply?" the desk clerk asked.

"Definitely. Tell Ms….uh...Sommers I'll be there. And thank you."

"Hot damn!" Dakota whooped, dancing around the room. "Looks like she didn't forget me. Okay, settle down, Dakota. What are you going to wear? Something nice, of course. Crap! I don't have much with me."

Eventually, she settled on a pair of relatively new Levi's and a pullover burgundy sweater.

"Well, at least she can't say I overdressed," she chuckled the following morning as she scowled at her image in the full-length mirror.

Yemaya was reading the newspaper in Le Castillion Restaurant when Dakota entered the room. Sensing her arrival, Yemaya looked up in time to see the head waiter pointing in her direction. Dressed in snug dark jeans and a burgundy sweater, Dakota looked extremely desirable. Standing, Yemaya smiled at her as she neared the table.

"Good morning, Dakota."

"Good morning, Yem...Jennifer. How are you doing?" Dakota sat in the chair nearest Yemaya. "And how is the leg?"

"The leg is much better, thank you. The stitches are out and no scarring."

"Really? You've healed already?"

"Pretty much. I heal quickly," Yemaya said nonchalantly.

"Apparently. So I know you have a show in three days, but I don't see anything scheduled after that."

"I will be returning home for a few months."

For some odd reason, Dakota felt a momentary loss. Looking down, she clutched her hands together under the table before raising her eyes to look at Yemaya.

"You must be excited about seeing your homeland again," she said unenthusiastically.

"I enjoy being with my friends and family," Yemaya agreed, watching the blonde woman closely. Her disappointment had not escaped her.

"Well, I hope you have a good stay," Dakota said, trying to sound more excited.

"Thank you. So what have you been doing since my last debacle?" Yemaya smirked, changing the subject.

"Oh, still doing research for my article. You're the last on my list, so I guess I'll be heading back home after the show. My boss is getting anxious about the article, so I need to at least give him a few details about its content."

Yemaya motioned for the waiter to bring coffee and croissants before commenting.

"What exactly is he expecting?"

"Some sensational exposé would be wonderful, but I think it'll be more about the lives of illusionists. Nothing really great, but it'll give the readers something to think about."

"Hmm...I know we have just met," Yemaya said, hesitantly, "but I have a proposition for you."

"Sounds interesting already. What's up?" Dakota asked, her curiosity piqued.

"I was wondering if you would like to join me for a few weeks at my home."

"You mean in Moldova?" Dakota was stunned at the invitation.

"Well, Taraclia, to be exact."

"Taraclia? I've never heard of it."

"Few people outside of our country have. It is a small town."

"It all sounds so...I don't know...exotic," Dakota replied, overwhelmed.

Yemaya laughed.

"Not even close. You can think about it and let me know in the next few days. I may even give you an interview," Yemaya teased, her blue eyes twinkling with laughter.

"How could I refuse such an interesting proposition? But won't I need a visa and tickets?"

"Normally, yes. But as my guest, entry is not a problem. I have chartered a jet to take me—us—there. The flight is about eleven hours by air, and we leave immediately after the performance. Bring your bags to the theater. I can make arrangements to have you picked up if you wish."

"That would be great. Anything special I'll need?"

"Not that I can think of."

The conversation was suddenly interrupted by a quiet melody. Reaching down, Yemaya pulled a cell phone from her jacket pocket. Excusing herself for the interruption, she flipped it open.

"Allo, Raidon. No, you are not interrupting me, but I am with someone. We will speak English so as not to appear rude. Yes, I will be bringing someone back...a guest...No, I see no need for that."

Dakota looked around the restaurant, trying not to eavesdrop. Finally giving up, she listened quietly as Yemaya conversed with the other party. It quickly became evident she was the main topic being discussed.

"No, Raidon, that will not be necessary. Just do as I say on this matter. Understand? Good...we should be there in a few days. Please warn the children of our arrival, otherwise they are sure to cause problems for my guest...The room next to mine will be fine...Fine...We can talk more when I get home...And to you too, brother."

Putting the phone away, she looked at Dakota.

"My brother. He can be very pushy at times," Yemaya said.

Dakota barely heard Yemaya's comment. Her mind focused on the word children, and she was stunned. Was Yemaya married? The thought caused her stomach to knot. She had felt a connection with the other woman. If she was married, grandmother Dakota was wrong.

What am I doing? It was only a dream. Her thoughts were interrupted by a hand touching hers.

"Dakota, is everything all right?" Yemaya asked, her concern evident.

"Uh...oh, yeah...just thinking about Grandma Dakota," Dakota replied, in an attempt to avoid what was actually bothering her. "I'm sorry. Did you say something?"

"Nothing important. Is something bothering you about your great-great-grandmother? You seem...distracted."

"No, not really. Just a silly dream I had yesterday."

"Maybe you should tell me about it. Anything dealing with Grandma Dakota has to be worth listening to."

Dakota related the dream, leaving out the more intimate details. Yemaya listened intently, amused at the animated description.

It was obvious from the red cheeks that she wasn't telling everything, but after having experienced her own dream about the elder Dakota, Yemaya suspected Dakota's held some rather interesting details the younger woman was too embarrassed to disclose.

When Dakota finished, Yemaya sat back in her chair, analyzing the details of the dream. It wasn't necessarily strange they both dreamt about the same woman, considering the earlier conversation. What puzzled her was that the grandmother called her magic woman in both dreams and discussed the threat of some darkness. When she got home, she would talk to Raidon. Perhaps he would have an answer.

Leaning forward, she placed her hand gently over Dakota's and squeezed it.

"It would seem your elder has been busy. I too met her in a dream. She looks very much like you."

"You dreamt of my grandmother? When? What happened in it? What did she say?"

"It was similar to yours. Mine was in a meadow covered in flowers. She seemed to be chanting but came over and talked with me. She called me magic woman and talked about a darkness coming."

"This has to be a little more than coincidence, doesn't it?" Dakota asked, frowning slightly.

"I agree. Perhaps once we get to Moldova, we might discover a little more."

Looking at her watch, Yemaya sighed.

"Unfortunately, I have to leave now. Perhaps you can join me for dinner later this evening."

"Sounds like a plan. I don't have anything else to do while I'm here."

"Good, I will send a car for you about seven. Now I need to prepare the staff for the show."

"I'll catch you later. Bye."

The two women stood simultaneously. Without thinking, Yemaya reached over and brushed some bangs from Dakota's eyes.

"You have beautiful hair," she remarked. Smiling, she stepped past the shocked woman and walked from the room. It took Dakota several minutes before she could bring herself to leave the restaurant. The innocent action of the other woman left her hot and flustered.

You're right, Grandma. She'd be something else in bed, Dakota thought. *I think I'm having an orgasm just thinking about it*. She shook her head when soft laughter flowed gently through her mind.

Chapter Six

The next two days, Yemaya and Dakota made it a point to eat breakfast together and dinner whenever possible. Yemaya would go to the theater while Dakota returned to her room to work on her article. Her boss was ecstatic when he heard she'd be joining Yemaya on her return to her homeland. He immediately offered her additional funds to cover any out-of-pocket expenses she might incur.

The day of the performance, Dakota packed her bag. Yemaya ordered a limousine to pick her up an hour before the show started. She was escorted backstage for a short visit, then to her seat.

Dakota tried to discover a few trade secrets while she was behind the curtains, but there wasn't anything unusual in the way of apparatus or special effects. In fact, the whole area was curiously empty except for a few fans and the scenery. The crew was busy preparing for Yemaya's performance, so she was being ignored.

As Yemaya stepped onto the stage, her eyes searched out Dakota. Once located, she nodded slightly and smiled. Her attention then returned to the audience and the show began.

Her theme was based on a story about a demon searching for souls. Dressed in a tight black and flame-colored body suit, Yemaya made a magnificent demon. The mask was shaped and colored like flames. As she strolled across the stage, her body suit shimmered, her fluid movements making the design flicker like real fire. Several members of the crew were dressed as minor demons or angels, all battling for souls. Yemaya would move toward a particular victim, circle it menacingly, her laughter wild in a cold, maniacal way. With a wave of her left hand, the lost soul was surrounded in a gray swirling mist.

Within seconds, it vanished along with the soul. The area surrounding the victim remained clear so the audience had full view of everything happening. The demon continued capturing angel and demon souls until few were left. Suddenly from above, a figure appeared, dressed in a white and gold body suit. Large feathered wings flapped slowly, lowering the archangel to the stage floor.

Her face was hidden behind an iridescent golden mask. Golden hair, almost waist length, flowed around her shoulders, breasts, and back. Thunder rolled and lightning flashed when she pointed her right hand at the demon. With a slight flick of her wrist, bluish flames burst upward from the stage floor and surrounded the Illusionist, concealing the lower half of her body. Writhing in agony, she screamed so realistically the audience shuddered, unsure of what was real or pretend. The archangel raised both arms toward the heavens, crossed them at the wrists, and bowed her head.

The demon threw orange balls of flame at her foe, but they merely disintegrated on some invisible barrier. Two puffs of grayish white smoke bellowed around her and the demon. A demoniacal howl broke the stillness. Within seconds, the smoke cleared. The demon was gone.

The crowd gasped, their eyes locked on the spot the Illusionist had been standing. It wasn't until the archangel turned to look at the audience that the members became aware the golden-haired woman had also disappeared.

In her place, dressed in the outfit of the angel stood Yemaya. Soon, the stage was filled with the lost souls and angels that had been vanquished. Clapping and cheering wildly, the audience members rose to their feet, impressed and yet unable to explain what they had just seen.

Two assistants approached Yemaya and removed the wings attached to her back. The harness was a complicated system of belts and buckles and cables, concealed by feathers. The process took several minutes, adding to the audience's awareness of the difficulty involved in putting on the costume. It would be impossible to slip into the outfit during the seconds she was hidden by the smoke.

Once free of the gear, Yemaya walked toward the edge of the stage and bowed. It took another five minutes for the crowd to settle down enough so she could be heard.

"Ladies and gentlemen, once again, I thank you for honoring me with your presence this evening. My shows are always inspired by your appreciation and enthusiasm. In today's world, we have little time to believe in such things as magic or the unsolved mysteries of the world. We are so caught up in work or politics or personal problems, we do not take the time to stop and wonder about the miraculous things around us. I hope tonight I inspired you in some way to rethink your lives and remember those joys and mysteries.

"This is my last performance for a while. I will be returning to my homeland to be with my own family. As always, my thoughts will be with you, my supporters. May all of you enjoy happiness and peace in your lives. Thank you."

Walking toward the side stage, she stopped to look for Dakota, who had been as mesmerized by the show as everyone else. Realizing Yemaya was looking at her, she gave a thumbs-up and smiled radiantly. Yemaya felt her heart skip a beat at the sight of the other woman's overwhelming approval. Returning the smile, she again stepped toward the curtain.

It was then the fine hair on Yemaya's arms and neck stood on end as if disturbed by static electricity. Stopping, she turned again toward the audience, pretending to give them a final wave. Her eyes scanned the crowd, looking for the source of her unease. Eventually, her gaze locked on a small, balding man sitting in an aisle seat near the back row. Her eyes narrowed ominously.

Dakota could tell something was bothering Yemaya. Turning her head, she stared into the darkness trying to see what she was looking at. Unfortunately, it was far too dark for her to make out anything but shapes. She was about to turn back toward Yemaya when she noticed a shadow moving quickly up the stairs toward the exit. At the point it walked through the brightly lit exit, she recognized the man as the one who took the pictures during the Charleston show.

Frowning, she turned back to see Yemaya's reaction, but the woman had left the stage. Dakota didn't know what to think. Leaving her seat, she headed toward the stage's side entrance. She needed to talk with Yemaya about this man's attempts to photograph her the week before.

Eddy Jones waited patiently for the show to begin. Other than his attendance at the Charleston Aquarium, he had never seen a magic show. Watching her walk on stage in a magnificent demon costume, he was impressed by her powerfully built body. Interestingly, he had no sexual interest in the woman. As a photographer, Eddy appreciated beauty. Yemaya Lysanne was beauty personified.

The first time she hesitated on stage, he didn't think anything of it, but when her show ended and she stopped again to stare into the same area as before, he became curious about who had caught her attention. He could see the back of the woman's head but nothing else. Then she turned and looked directly at him.

"Shit," he muttered. "It's her. Chisholm isn't going to like this."

Scurrying from the room, he never noticed the cold gaze following him nor the slow hiss as Yemaya sensed his unnatural interest in Dakota. She would remember him.

Sweat poured down Eddy's face as he hailed a taxi to take him back to his hotel. He would have to think of something. If Chisholm guessed he'd lied, he was as dead as the woman in the subway.

Dakota caught up with Yemaya in her dressing room.

"What was that about?" she asked.

"What was what about?" Yemaya responded evasively.

"That man you were looking at. Who was he?"

"I do not know. Probably just a fan," she replied nonchalantly in an effort to drop the subject.

"Maybe," Dakota said, not willing to let the woman off so easily. "But I noticed him at your last performance. He was taking pictures."

"Really? Everyone was screened for electronic equipment."

"Yeah, I know. I thought at the time it was strange but figured he had just gotten special permission or something."

"No one gets special permission. No cameras means no cameras. Are you sure it was him?"

"Positive. Same size, same features, and balding. Something about him I don't like."

"Well, I can have him checked out. Should be simple to do since I know his seat number."

"How could you see where he was sitting? It was way too dark for me until he walked through the door."

"I have excellent night vision. Good genes, I guess," Yemaya explained, unwilling to discuss her skills further.

"Uh-huh. I see you're still closed-mouth about things that pertain to you," Dakota pouted, looking pitiful.

Laughing, Yemaya stood and gave the woman a warm hug.

"Poor baby. Maybe I can make it up to you once we arrive at my home. How much more personal can that be?"

"Well...there's personal...then there's *personal*," Dakota said, wiggling her eyebrows mischievously.

"Yes," Yemaya said, her voice low and seductive. "There most certainly is. Which are you interested in?"

Blushing, Dakota focused on the midriff of the woman just inches away from her.

"Um...well...um...hey! Isn't it about time we got a move on it? Chartering a jet can't be very cheap, and I bet they charge by the hour."

"Nice parry, Dakota. But this conversation is just being postponed, not ended," she warned. "Shall we go? As you say, time is money."

Gathering up their luggage, they left for the airport, both relieved at not having to pursue the conversation but feeling a little disappointed that some questions hadn't been answered.

Three days later, Eddy was standing in front of Robert Chisholm giving him an update on his investigation.

"That's right, Mr. Chisholm. Lysanne chartered a flight to her homeland the same night of the performance. A Dakota Devereaux is accompanying her."

"And exactly who is Dakota Devereaux?"

Smiling smugly, Eddy handed him a file.

"Jones, I don't have time to read your damn report. Just answer me."

"She's an employee of yours."

"Of mine? She works for me?"

"Well, not exactly. She works for a magazine you own. She's doing research on illusionists. Apparently, Lysanne was one of her subjects. Somehow, Devereaux caught her attention, and Lysanne must've offered her a visit to her homeland."

"Interesting. So by now they're in Moldova?"

"Yes, sir. My sources say they arrived early Saturday. At least their flight landed in Cahul."

"You have contacts in Moldova?" Chisholm asked.

"A few. I met some people from there when I was in Romania ten years ago. They needed help at the time, and I was more idealistic then. I made good money as a photographer, so I helped them get home, then set them up in a small business. They owed me a favor, so I called it in. I can tell you this, though. Honor is important to them. They were reluctant to talk about Lysanne or her family. The family seems to have a lot of influence in Moldova."

"Family?"

"Seems she has a brother. They are rather elite citizens in their country. They can come and go at will, and they command extreme loyalty from everyone around them. I couldn't get any more than that from Georgio."

"Good work, Jones. Now I want you to go over there with a few of my men and see what you can find out about her and her family."

"Mr. Chisholm, I don't know if I can get into Moldova."

"Call your friends. Offer them money or whatever else they want. Threaten them if you have to. I don't care how you do it but do it. You understand? Do what it takes. Now here's the information on who will be accompanying you."

"I'll see what I can do."

"Good. And, Jones, don't come back if you can't do this. You'll have no future here or anywhere. Now get out."

Eddy Jones was never more frightened in his life. He had sold his soul to the devil and now he was paying his dues. Robert Chisholm was fixated on the Illusionist, and nothing was going to prevent him from having her.

Chapter Seven

The plane landed in Moldova mid-morning. A chauffeur in a black Hummer was waiting at the airport to drive them to Yemaya's estate in Taraclia. The trip would take several hours traveling through the mountainous terrain. The estate was well secluded. First, however, Yemaya needed to pay her respects to some acquaintances in Cahul. A luncheon had been arranged for her and her guest.

Although Yemaya wasn't interested in meeting with the president of Moldova, manners dictated she at least attend the function. Her people had a special arrangement with the governmental parties of the country. They stayed out of politics as long as they were left to come and go as they wanted. The parties knew it was in their best interests to accommodate anyone associated with the Lysannes.

With their influence, they could easily choose who would run the country. The Lysannes, however, chose not to get involved, which was all the better for the party members. It also kept the majority fairly honest.

The luncheon lasted several hours. After learning Dakota was a journalist, everyone wanted to gain her favor. Amused, Yemaya sat back and silently watched the men and women vying for the young woman's attention so they could get their name in print. Dakota was less than thrilled. Finally, Yemaya decided to go to her rescue.

"Mr. President, Madame, I am afraid we have a long journey ahead of us, and I would like to get home by sunset.

I know you understand how treacherous the roads can be after dark."

"Yes, of course, Ms. Lysanne. It was a pleasure to see you again and to have met your beautiful young guest."

"It was my honor, Mr. President," Dakota interrupted, not liking how the man was talking around her. President or not, she wasn't invisible.

Back in the Hummer, Yemaya ordered her chauffeur to take them home.

Dakota was exhausted. Eventually, the warmth of the car and the long flight took its toll. Slipping into a quiet slumber, her head slid sideways until it rested against Yemaya's shoulder.

The sun slipped behind the mountains, its golden rays turning orange as it disappeared. Long shadows stretched across the road. Gusts of wind moved tree limbs, making the shadows dance back and forth. The howl of a wolf woke Dakota from a strange dream about ghosts and vampires. Shivering, she became aware of the soft shoulder beneath her cheek.

"Are you cold?" Yemaya asked, feeling the shiver.

"No, just a strange dream." Dakota straightened up and yawned.

"It is the mountains. They bring out people's fears, especially if you are not from this land."

"And if you are?"

"Then you know what is real and what is only imagination, hopefully," Yemaya replied solemnly.

"Are there things to fear here?"

"There are things to fear everywhere, Dakota. And to answer your question, yes, there is even here. We have our own demons in these lands. Most are two-legged, but occasionally, a few take other forms."

Dakota shivered again. This time, it wasn't from being cold or tired. She didn't consider herself superstitious. She always kept an open mind about things beyond reason or logic. Yemaya's comments seemed to hold a warning.

"Is there anything *you* are afraid of around here?" she asked uneasily.

Yemaya stared out the window for several minutes not sure how to answer. Finally, she turned back to Dakota.

"There are some things. My people occasionally speak about creatures of unspeakable evil. You will probably hear a few. Superstitions are hard to eliminate."

"My people? You make it sound like you're different from everyone else."

"We are," Yemaya smirked. "So be forewarned," she joked, nudging Dakota in the ribs. "After all, I did say you barely know me."

"That's true. Anything in particular I should be forewarned about?"

Putting the fingertips of her right hand against her cheek in a mock thinking pose, Yemaya looked toward the ceiling of the Hummer.

"Hmm...let me think. Do I want to scare you on your first day or take advantage of your innocence later?" she mused before looking at Dakota.

Dakota could have sworn Yemaya's eyes held an unnatural gleam. They seemed almost predatory.

"Do I get to choose?" Dakota asked, trying to keep the conversation light.

"You always have choices, Dakota. Which one would you choose?"

"Truthfully, you taking advantage of my innocence sounds rather interesting, but I think for now, I'll let you tell me some of your scary stories. You have any I may have heard when I was growing up? This *is* werewolf country, isn't it?" she teased.

"No, dear. That is the other side of the mountains," Yemaya countered. "Now let me think. I suppose the most well-known legend is Count Dracula."

"I thought he was from Transylvania. You're not from there, are you?"

"Not really. But close enough."

"Was he really a vampire?"

Shrugging, Yemaya again looked out the window, pale eyes scanning the shadows

"No, just a madman."

"So are there such things?"

"Who can say? The word has been around a long time."

"Well, I'd hate to think they existed."

"I would not be too anxious to meet one myself," Yemaya replied seriously. "There are too many other things to fear without adding them to the list."

"I suppose so," Dakota agreed. "How long before we arrive?"

"Two minutes." Leaning across Dakota, Yemaya pointed out the window. Dakota caught her breath as the other woman's breasts brushed against her. For a moment, ice blue eyes stared warmly into hers, causing her to blush, then Yemaya winked, ducked her head slightly, and nodded toward the horizon.

Dakota saw a large stone structure rising from the ground. Turrets on both sides and a huge drawbridge spanning a narrow river gave her the impression of an old English castle. Because the night air cooled rapidly, a mist rose from the warmer waters of the river, giving it an almost haunted look.

"Wow! You never said you lived in a castle," Dakota exclaimed, awestruck.

"I would not exactly call it a castle. More an unusually shaped stone house. It has been in my family for over six hundred years."

"It's a castle to me."

"Maybe so. Andrei, please stop the car on this side of the bridge. Ms. Devereaux and I will walk the rest of the way."

"As you wish, mistress." The chauffeur stopped the Hummer and opened the door for his boss. "I'll take the luggage through the back."

"Thank you. Please let Maria know we will have dinner in the small guest room."

"Yes, ma'am"

Pointing toward the drawbridge, Yemaya nodded, slightly sweeping her arm toward the castle.

"After you."

Dakota stepped hesitantly onto the wooden timbers that formed the base of the drawbridge. Each beam was over ten inches thick and twenty feet long and was held tightly together by forged steel bands and bolts. With the bridge over thirty feet long, Dakota couldn't imagine how anyone could raise it.

"It was only raised if it needed to be," Yemaya explained, picking up on Dakota's thoughts. "The last time that happened was about five hundred years ago. A local warlord decided to challenge my ancestors for the rights to the land. It was his last challenge. After his defeat, no one else bothered us."

"You make it sound rather ominous," Dakota responded, trying to imagine what it was like in those times.

"Sorry. It's a part of my history."

Dakota was about to respond when she was interrupted by the sound of baying wolves. From the dense forest surrounding the estate, she saw several animals charging toward them.

"Yemaya!" she screamed, pointing to the wolves. In an unconscious effort to shield the other woman, Dakota jumped in front of Yemaya. She had no idea what she would do, but she knew she would do whatever it took to protect Yemaya.

Yemaya was so startled by Dakota's actions, it took her a moment to react. Then she stepped forward and motioned to the five wolves. Immediately, they halted panting, their tongues lolling from their mouths. Yemaya knelt on one knee. A female wolf slowly approached, her eyes gleaming brightly in the moonlight. Lips curled upward, exposing enormous teeth, and a low growl rumbled from her throat.

"Yemaya," Dakota whispered, watching the pack closely. "Those...those are wolves. Be careful."

Yemaya stretched out her hand, palm down. The female bent her head and rubbed her forehead against the palm. As if a sign, the remainder of the pack dashed in, knocking the woman to the ground.

Dakota immediately jumped in and grabbed one of the wolves by the fur, trying to pull it off Yemaya. The wolf spun, lunging at her, fangs bared.

"Cushna. Ho! Prieten!" Yemaya yelled. "Scalciat!"

The wolf dropped as if shot. The rest of the wolves backed off and lay down. Getting up, Yemaya brushed the dirt from her trousers. Laughing softly, she took Dakota by the arm and pulled her forward.

"Sorry, Dakota. Let me introduce you to my 'children.'"

"Children? You call these children? They're wolves!" Her voice trembled from the shock of the near attack.

"Yes, they are, but they are friends, too. At least I think of them as my children since I raised their grandmother and great-grandmother before them. This is Regina. She is the alpha female and the leader of the pack. Voinic here is her mate. His name means Prince Charming. He loves to be loved, although he acts indifferent." Yemaya ruffled his fur. "Her three offspring are Tandru Simtire, which means gentle soul; Tanc, or brat; and Clovn, clown."

Calling each wolf forward, one by one, she introduced them to Dakota. All but Tandru Simtire simply sniffed at her, then backed away. The young female wolf seemed more curious, though. Sniffing at Dakota's hand, she then set about inspecting the rest of her. Apparently satisfied, the wolf sat and stared into her eyes. Dakota stood transfixed, unable to look away. It was obvious the animal was highly intelligent.

Yemaya watched the wolf closely. She wasn't sure how they were going to react to Dakota. Rarely did they make an appearance when strangers were around, but their bond with Yemaya was so strong, their excitement so great, they couldn't resist the need to be with her.

"Simtire likes you."

"How can you tell? Maybe she's just trying to figure out what part of me she would like to eat first," Dakota said, maintaining contact with the young wolf.

"Well, first, she is a wolf. She does not eat people. Second, if she did not like you, she would have backed off. As for eating you, now there is a thought," Yemaya joked, wiggling her eyebrows suggestively.

Blushing, Dakota tried to ignore the images racing through her mind. The temperature outside seemed to be getting a lot warmer.

"Oh, great! So the others don't like me, huh?" she asked, trying to keep the conversation on the wolves.

"Did I say that?" Yemaya laughed, aware that Dakota's heartbeat had increased considerably and decided to go easy on her. "Actually, they take longer to make up their minds. But you have no reason to fear them. Should the need arise, they will even protect you," she stated matter-of-factly.

"That's comforting," Dakota said, turning slowly to look at Yemaya. "Can we go in now? I *think* I may need to use your bathroom," she joked halfheartedly.

Laughing, Yemaya turned toward the wolves and waved her hands toward the woods.

"A se duce!"

The wolves immediately jumped up and ran toward the woods, bouncing and playing like overexuberant kids.

"Bathroom it is," Yemaya smirked

Both women turned at the sound of approaching footsteps.

"Good evening, brother," Yemaya said, turning toward the tall figure standing in the shadows a few feet away.

"Good evening. I hope your trip was uneventful."

"Quite. Shall we go inside before I make the proper introductions?"

Raidon stepped aside, allowing the two women to pass. Once inside, he motioned them toward the study.

"Shortly, brother. I think Dakota needs to freshen up a bit first."

"Of course. If you will excuse me." Bowing slightly, he disappeared behind a large wooden door.

Ten minutes later, the two women joined Raidon. A small fire blazed in the oversized fireplace recessed in the far wall. Shadows flickered as the flames danced across the wooden logs. Yemaya led Dakota to a soft leather couch, pushing her gently down before sitting next to her. Raidon walked to a large chair and sat, crossing his right leg over his left.

"So, sister. Be so kind as to introduce me to your young friend," he ordered.

Raising an eyebrow, she stared at her brother. He could be so pompous sometimes. Raidon smirked and acknowledged her thoughts with a nod.

"Certainly. Dakota, this is my brother, Raidon Lysanne. Raidon, Dakota Devereaux, my friend."

"A pleasure, Ms. Devereaux. Yemaya tells me you are a journalist. Perhaps I have read some of your work."

"Probably not, Mr. Lysanne, and the name is Dakota."

"As you wish, Dakota, and I am simply Raidon. You must be exhausted from your trip. Would you like to rest before joining us for dinner?"

Dakota got the impression Raidon wished to talk with his sister alone. Rising to her feet, she nodded.

"Actually, if someone would show me my room, I'd like to unpack a few things."

"I will show you to your room and the facilities, Dakota. Excuse us, brother," Yemaya said.

"Take your time. I have several reports to look over."

Standing, Raidon bowed to the women before leaving the room.

"Is he always so formal?" Dakota asked.

"Always," Yemaya laughed. "But he can be so much fun to tease. I have only seen him relax around Reymone, his confidant. Now let me show you to your room."

Once Dakota was settled in, Yemaya went to the study. Raidon was sitting by the fire reading a local newspaper. Once she was seated, he looked up.

"You are looking well. Does it have anything to do with the young woman ?"

"What is your point, Raidon?"

"Just curious. You have never brought anyone to our homeland before, other than Sonny. I'm just wondering what this woman means to you. As a journalist, she is a threat to our people," he stated calmly.

"As a *friend*, she is a guest in our home. As a *guest*, she will be accorded our hospitality *and* our protection. And as to what she is to me, that is my business."

"I have responsibilities, Yemaya. While you travel the world, I must take care of business here. Any stranger in our household *is* my business."

"Within limits. My limits. Understand me, brother. My guest is none of your business. Do I make myself clear?" she demanded coldly.

Laughing, Raidon smiled broadly.

"You always make yourself perfectly clear. I've always respected your wishes. I have to admit, she's quite charming and very attractive. I'm not surprised you find her desirable."

"She is a friend, Raidon. Nothing more," Yemaya said.

"Whatever you say," Raidon replied, smiling knowingly. "Now to business. Sonny hasn't been able to find out any information about what happened to the platform. He has tracked down a few leads through government sources and discovered a man named Eddy Jones has been asking questions about you. Your young friend has been checking on you, too, it seems."

"She is a journalist. Of course she asks questions. She is working on an article about magicians and illusionists."

"I have no doubt she is exactly who she says she is. I merely commented on her name coming up also. It seems she has a curious connection with this Jones fellow."

"In what way?" Yemaya demanded, leaning forward, her elbows resting on her knees.

"Well, Sonny says Jones works for a man named Robert Chisholm. Mr. Chisholm is the CEO of Wentworth Publications, who in turn owns the magazine Ms. Devereaux works for. A rather strange coincidence, wouldn't you agree?"

"Merely coincidence and nothing more," Yemaya said dismissively. "Anything else?"

"It seems Jones attended a few of your performances."

Raidon handed Yemaya several snapshots. She looked at the photo, immediately recognizing him as the man she saw at the Montreal show.

"He was at my last performance. Dakota said he was also trying to take pictures of me in Charleston. It would seem he has been busy."

"So it appears. We tracked his movements from Miami to Charleston the day of the show. Then he went to Atlanta the weekend after your show and back to Miami Monday night. A trip to Montreal for your show, and now it seems he has again returned to Miami. This man definitely gets around."

"But why the trip to Atlanta?"

"Perhaps this may have something to do with it."

Raidon handed her a news clipping about a woman killed in the MARTA subway. Had it not been for the remark about her attending Yemaya's show, no one would have made the connection.

"Sonny is really good. Remind me to give him a raise," Yemaya said. "So how does Brenda Simpson fit into this?"

"I'm not sure. She attended the Charleston performance but has no apparent connections with anyone. We're still trying to figure that out. Perhaps you might see something we haven't. Take a look through the folder and see if something jogs your memory."

Nodding, Yemaya leaned back and opened the blue folder. Several more pictures of Eddy Jones were in the file. Two photos of an attractive older woman were under Jones's. Blonde hair, blue eyes, and dimples made her think of Dakota. It wasn't until she picked up Sonny's detailed report on Ms. Simpson that she felt uneasy. Brenda Simpson had been sitting one row behind Dakota's aisle. She was also one seat number off.

"Raidon, when Dakota told me she saw a man fitting Jones's description, she said he was trying to take pictures. She looked directly at him when she saw the flash. Once he realized she had seen him, he left in a hurry."

"So, you think he was after Dakota and got the wrong woman? Question is, why would he kill Dakota just because she saw him?"

"Why indeed. But it would seem a possibility. If he does want her dead, he might make another attempt."

"I don't think that's likely, Yemaya. Why would he connect her with you?"

"Because Dakota was at my last show. When I was walking off stage, I stopped to look at her. I was about to step behind the curtains when I felt a presence, something sinister. That is when I saw this Jones character at the back of the theater. He was looking directly at Dakota. I could feel his fear, Raidon, and something more. He wanted her dead. I would have killed him then had there not been so many people present," his sister growled.

"Most unlike you, sister," Raidon chuckled, amused at the unusual emotions Yemaya was displaying. "But I don't think Dakota is in danger here."

"Probably not," she agreed. Her people would not betray any member of her family or their friends. Still there were others who could be bought for the right price. No place was completely safe. Sensing Dakota walking toward the study door, she handed Raidon the file.

"We will not speak of this to Dakota. At least not yet."

"As you wish. But I think your young woman is quite capable of taking care of herself under normal circumstances," he commented unexpectedly.

"These are not normal circumstances. Until we find out what drives Jones, we keep this quiet."

A light knock on the door interrupted Raidon's response.

"Come in, Dakota," Raidon said, standing when she entered the room. "I trust your accommodations are satisfactory."

"My room is beautiful, Raidon. Thank you."

"Good. Then we can eat. You will lead the way, Yemaya?"

Dinner was a combination of salads, steamed vegetables, a strange sweet potato dish, cheeses, and fresh bread. It seemed a strange combination, but everything was seasoned and served with sweet butter and homemade dressing. After sampling each dish, Dakota felt pleasantly full.

"This was delicious," she said, her praise genuine. "Do you always eat like this?"

"Like this?" Raidon asked.

"I noticed no meat," Dakota said. "Not that I'm complaining."

"Ah, yes. We rarely eat meat."

"Are you vegetarians?"

"No, we have our moments. But for the most part, we stick with this style of food. Do you wish meat at your next meal? I can have the cook prepare a nice cut of veal or lamb for you."

"No, I kind of like this. I don't feel so stuffed," Dakota replied, patting her stomach. "Besides, I just might lose a few pounds on this diet," she joked.

"You are fine just the way you are, Dakota."

Blushing again, Dakota looked directly at Yemaya. "Thank you. Do you mind if I call it a night? I'm rather tired from the trip." As if to confirm her exhaustion, she barely had time to hide her yawn with her hand.

"I think an early night would be good for me, too. Will you excuse us, Raidon?"

"Of course. Sleep well Dakota, sister."

Chapter Eight

Eddy Jones arrived in Cahul with Chisholm's three henchmen. It had taken a lot of persuasion and $50,000 to get his contacts to agree to help him. Another $10,000 expedited the paperwork. The visas arrived a few days later.

Once in Cahul, he managed to find a few sketchy details about Yemaya's whereabouts, at least the town near her home. No one was eager to disclose where she lived, only that he should go to Taraclia. He was given a contact, the name of a local man who would assist them further. Another $5,000.

Chisholm didn't question Eddy's continual need for funds. He was well aware of the difficulty in getting cooperation in Moldova. The fact Jones had gotten as far as he had was impressive. Perhaps he underestimated the little man's abilities.

The ride to Taraclia was long and monotonous. Eddy rented two local vehicles to make them less conspicuous. The group traveled together until they arrived at the town limits. Then Eddy gave the three men the address of a local motel with orders to stay there and keep a low profile. Afterward, he drove to his contact's house.

A middle-aged woman with graying hair answered the door. Stepping back, she motioned Eddy in and led him to a chair in the kitchen before leaving the room. Minutes later, a large fat man walked in, his head covered in the local headgear. A long beard, thick eyebrows, and a scar running through his right brow and down his right cheek gave him a sinister appearance.

"Good evening, Mr. Jones. We have business to discuss, yes?"

"If you are Vlamick, then yes," Eddy responded, handing him a brown envelope. "I believe this is the price you quoted for your services."

Tucking the envelope in his wide waistband, Vlamick smiled.

"I have arranged for you and your friends to take a small ride tomorrow. The cost is only five hundred American dollars for your guide. A bargain."

"I just paid you for your services," Eddy growled.

"True, Mr. Jones," Vlamick said, spreading his arms wide apologetically. "But the rest of the money is for the services of the guide. As you can see, I am not a young man anymore. I cannot go walking through the mountains like I did in my youth. You perhaps do not wish a guide. I can always point you in the direction of Ms. Lysanne's home, but I think you may get lost in our forests, and there are things there you do not wish to meet up with, I promise you."

"No, I'll pay," Eddy said, reaching into his jacket pocket and pulling out enough money to cover the additional expense. "I *hope* this will be the last charge, Vlamick. My boss doesn't like surprises. You know what I mean?" he threatened.

"I cannot be responsible because others wish to take advantage of opportunities, Mr. Jones. Your boss will have to pay whatever it costs if he wishes to ensure our cooperation. We are taking great risks by assisting you. I'm sure you can appreciate the value of those risks."

Eddy decided to let the subject drop. It wouldn't help his cause to alienate the one contact he had in Taraclia. Later, he would deal with the Moldovan.

"I get your point. What is the plan for tomorrow?"

"My guide will pick you up at your motel. He will drive you into the hillside a short distance. Then you will have to walk a few miles to reach Ms. Lysanne's home. The woods are cold, so you will need to dress appropriately."

"Why can't we just drive a short distance from her place and walk in?" Eddy demanded.

"You would be noticed and questioned. They are suspicious people, the Lysannes. There is only one road in and out. This is the only way you can get close enough to see the house. Even then, you will need binoculars. Be prepared to spend the night. My guide will have everything you need."

"Fuck," Eddy muttered. Communing with nature was not his idea of a good time. "Okay. We'll be waiting for your guide. Oh, and, Vlamick, I may need your services again. It could require...um...transporting a large package out of your country. Not through normal routes, if you know what I mean."

"Of course, It can be arranged...for a price naturally." Vlamick grinned.

"Naturally," Eddy said, taking his leave.

Yemaya only agreed to let Dakota go for walks by herself if she took Simtire with her. It was obvious the young wolf adored her, which was unusual. Wolves normally did not bond so easily with humans.

The morning after their arrival at the castle, as Dakota called it, she and Yemaya walked along the river. The weather was brisk. A breeze blew down the mountains and followed the river, adding to the coolness. After traveling a short distance, Yemaya directed Dakota onto a well-worn path disappearing into the forest. Once amongst the trees, the sun barely made it through the canopy, making it colder than the riverbank. They slowly climbed to a ridge overlooking the treetops, the river, and Yemaya's home. Hills and small mountains covered the landscape as far as the eye could see.

A grayish-white haze cloaked the valley, giving it a ghostly aura.

"Taraclia is beyond that ridge," Yemaya said, pointing toward the south. "It is best known for its wine industry, but there are some people who want to bring in some light industrial plants."

"Is there a chance of that happening?"

"It is possible but not likely. Some industry is necessary, but my people will not let it endanger the land."

"That's the second time you've said 'my people,' as if you're different from others here," Dakota observed, curious about the strange phrasing.

"I am," Yemaya replied. "My people are Carpi."

"Like the mountains," Dakota commented.

"Yes, our ancestors settled this area long before other tribes moved here. We are close to the land but willing to share its resources and bounty as long as they did not abuse it or our generosity."

Dakota was amazed at the intense emotion behind Yemaya's words. Obviously, she was proud of her heritage and was accepting of some change, but she held a steely conviction against those who sought to take advantage of the land or her people.

"You sound as if you would actually do something terrible if you didn't like some of the changes here."

"Terrible? No, but we will do what is necessary to protect all that we hold sacred," Yemaya said. "My people choose not to enter into politics but only as long as the government leaves us alone and does not abuse its political position."

"There are *that* many of you?"

"There are only a few of us, but we do have *that* much power," Yemaya answered quietly, turning to look at the woman standing next to her.

"You must be extremely wealthy then," Dakota said.

"We are comfortable, but money only makes life easier. It cannot solve the greater problems."

"So I take it money isn't what you mean by power. I hope you aren't into anything criminal or nefarious," Dakota joked.

Yemaya laughed, amused as the image of herself in a black suit with a black hat pulled low over her eyes..

"I assure you we are not mafia. No godfathers, no hit men. We have no need for that. We are more...subtle."

"Subtle...hmm...an interesting word. Okay, I give up. How can a minority control a majority without the use of money and/or force?" Dakota asked, her hands on her hips.

Yemaya cocked her head and stared at Dakota. She was intrigued by her inquisitive mind, not to mention very attracted to her on other levels. Aware Dakota felt the same way, she wanted to take her time pursuing the relationship.

Dakota needed to know her as a person and a Carpi, an ancient people with very few modern-day descendants. Rumored to have existed long before the pyramids of Egypt were built, it was believed some could read minds and control them, even shift shapes. As with all legends, there was some truth in them, but most rumors were the products of overactive imaginations. The majority of her people chose to remain near the homeland, only venturing beyond their borders for business or holidays.

"Well, you might say we can be very *persuasive* at times," she smirked.

Dakota snorted derisively.

"Persuasive. There's a word to put fear in people," she mused.

"If needed," Yemaya agreed. "You would be surprised at the power persuasion holds. Think about all the people who have been persuaded to do things they find abhorrent. Wars, fanatical religions, prejudices, hatred are all the byproducts of persuasion."

After thinking about it, Dakota nodded in agreement.

"I suppose so...in a way. But you'd have to be able to influence people on a very grand scale to convince an entire population or its government."

"True. But it is not as hard as you might think. The best example might be World War II. When Hitler rose to power, was it not his ability to 'connect' with his people that made him their leader?"

"You know, most people would say you lost the argument by bringing him into the conversation," Dakota joked.

"I suppose if we were arguing, you would be right. My point is, he was a very persuasive man, able to convince his people to destroy millions of lives. Would that not epitomize the power of persuasion?"

"I see what you mean. He wouldn't by chance have Carpi blood in his lineage, would he?"

"None we have been able to trace, but we have always sought knowledge. Many have left the homeland over the millennium. Most returned, but others choose to live elsewhere. It is possible they found partners and passed on our genes."

"So others may have your abilities?"

"More than possible, Dakota. It is inevitable. That is one reason my brother and I travel so much. We search for anyone of Carpi blood who has our abilities and make sure they do no serious harm."

Staring at the scenic view in front of her, Dakota turned slowly to look at Yemaya.

"Do no serious harm? That sounds rather ominous. What does it mean exactly?" she asked, disturbed by the phrase.

Yemaya stared at the river several hundred feet below. Taking a deep breath, she wondered if she'd said too much.

"It means exactly that. We cannot allow our people to put in motion events that might lead to another world war. The planet would not survive the next one. I realize it sounds like we are playing God, but we only try to prevent damage my people may do. Others we leave to fate."

"But if you have so much power, why not use it to bring about world peace? Use it on everyone and end all the misery?" Dakota queried, not sure she entirely believed any person or people were capable of so much control.

Running her fingers through her hair, Yemaya sighed.

"As much as we want peace, my people believe in letting destiny decide our fates," she stated, holding up her hand to stop the next logical question. "I know. Are we not interfering with destiny already? And the answer is yes but in a small way. We have special gifts. They were never meant for evil. If someone chooses to use them for that, we have an obligation to stop them. Normally, that means bringing them home. Occasionally, if the person has committed grave atrocities, he or she will be removed by whatever means necessary."

Shaking her head, Dakota held up her hand to halt the conversation for a moment.

"This is a lot to think about, Yemaya. I don't know whether to believe what you're saying, yet I feel it has to be true. It would explain so much about you and your skills. Do they have anything to do with your performances?"

Yemaya remained silent. As much as she liked Dakota, she was unwilling to disclose the secret to her illusions.

A sudden thought made Dakota step away from the taller woman.

"Do *you* ever use your ability to influence or control people?"

Yemaya caught the uncertainty in Dakota's voice. Stepping close to her, she put her hands on Dakota's shoulders and bent her knees so she was eye level with her. Holding her gaze, she shook her head slightly before answering in a low soft whisper.

"Not in the way you mean, Dakota. I would never do that just to satisfy a personal need. My attraction to you is real. Do you believe me?"

Nodding, Dakota sighed with relief.

"Good. You never need fear me."

Pulling her close, Yemaya tilted her head slightly and leaned forward until her lips brushed Dakota's. Dakota felt her arms raise, instinctively wrapping around the taller woman's neck, pulling her closer. Bending her head, Yemaya pressed her lips to Dakota's, the tip of her tongue caressing her lips.

Feeling the tentative touch, Dakota opened her mouth, giving Yemaya full access. Yemaya wrapped her arms around the smaller woman, pulling her body tightly against her own. The feel of breasts and hips pushing against her made her heart race. Dakota was overwhelmed, her own heart pounding furiously, all previous thoughts vanquished.

The sound of baying wolves caused both women to break off the kiss. Yemaya looked around, aware the animals had picked up on her confusion and were coming to her rescue. Dakota was just regaining her senses when she saw the pack moving warily toward them, hackles raised.

When Yemaya spoke, the wolves calmed down and the pack ran happily toward them. All but Simtire pounced on the taller woman. Simtire cautiously approached Dakota, lowering her body into a crawl. Recognizing the animal's subservient gesture, Dakota knelt down, extending her hand, palm up.

"Come on, pretty girl," she whispered softly. Immediately, Simtire jumped up and launched herself at Dakota, knocking her backward onto her butt. The next thing Dakota knew, she was being thoroughly cleaned by a long wet tongue as the young wolf straddled her lap. Laughing, she grabbed the fur around her neck and began wrestling with the wolf. Caught up in their roughhousing, neither noticed the others had stopped to watch. Yemaya was amused and the pack curious about Simtire's decision to ignore the mistress for a stranger.

Eventually, Dakota grew tired from the physical activity. Simtire sensed the change and backed off. Sitting a few feet away, her tongue draped from the side of her mouth, large canine teeth displayed in a wolfish grin.

"I see you have imprinted yourself on Simtire."

"Imprinted?" Dakota asked, ruffling the gray hair around the wolf's neck.

"A way of saying she has bonded with you. It is an honor."

"She's beautiful, isn't she?"

"Quite beautiful."

Looking up, Dakota had the impression Yemaya wasn't talking about the wolf.

"Um...guess we need to be getting back, huh?" she asked, suddenly feeling embarrassed.

"Good idea," Yemaya agreed.

FRAN HECKROTTE

Chapter Nine

The guide spoke very little English. Most of his communication was by hand signals, otherwise he rarely said anything. Motioning the three men into an old beatup van, he headed into the hills. The shaking and rattling of the van, along with the loud engine noise, quickly made everyone irritable.

"When are we going to reach this fuckin' broad's place?" Jimmy demanded. "Chisholm must be out of his fuckin' mind to be sending us halfway around the world for some bitch. I don't care how good lookin' she is."

"Shut up, Jimmy," snapped Billy, the older of the three. "You're always bitchin' about something, and I'm tired of listening to it."

"Don't go tellin' me to shut up, you asshole. You're the one who talked me into coming here. Said I'd make some good money and all I needed to do was grab this bitch and get her out of this piss ant-sized country. Well, no one said I'd have to live like some fuckin' freak trying to commune with nature," he sneered.

Eddy and Chuck said nothing. Best to let them get it out of their systems before they started the hike to Yemaya's home. Otherwise, they'd have to listen to the bickering for a long time. Eventually, the two men dozed, giving Eddy a chance to talk to Chuck.

"You understand our job, right?" Eddy asked.

"Yeah, Chisholm wants us to snatch this broad and run. Can't figure out why he waits till she's halfway around the planet to go after her. It would've been easier back in the States."

"Not in this case. She seems to have an extremely good security network, although we haven't figured out exactly how it works. Chisholm figures if she's in her own environment, she'll be more relaxed and more vulnerable."

"Well, Jimmy's right about one thing. He's fuckin' nuts. All this money and trouble. Ain't no woman worth this much trouble."

"Seems Chisholm thinks otherwise. I don't know why he's after Lysanne, but he seems to have a hard-on for her for some reason. It's cost him over a hundred grand already, and we're as close as anyone has gotten to her. If we don't bring her back, we might as well stay right here in Moldova 'cause there won't be anywhere else on the planet safe from him. He's about as crazy as anyone I've ever met."

They were interrupted by the guide stopping the van. Motioning for everyone to get out, he unloaded the packs from the back of the vehicle. Pointing to the equipment, he assigned each man a pack and bedroll, then walked off into the woods. Cursing, the four men grabbed the bags and followed. It wasn't until dusk that the guide halted, motioning for the men to make camp.

"Kerc, how much farther to our goal?" Eddy asked the guide.

"Tomorrow," Kerc replied as he spread a blanket on the ground. Sitting, he reached into his pack, pulled out some dried mutton, and began chewing.

"You don't expect us to eat that crap, do you?" Jimmy demanded. "I ain't eatin' that shit."

"You eat. No fire," the guide ordered.

"Fuck you. It's bad enough we have to spend the night here, but I ain't stayin' out here without some type of heat or light."

"No fire," Kerc repeated.

Ignoring the order, Jimmy bent down to pick up a piece of firewood. The thud of a knife sticking in the ground within inches of his hand made him jump backward.

"What the fuck?" he yelled, turning toward the guide. "I'll kill you, you fuckin' asshole."

Smiling, the guide shrugged, unimpressed.

"Maybe so. Then you all die. Now I sleep."

Rolling onto his side, he quickly fell asleep. Mumbling, Jimmy turned toward the rest of the group for support. The others just shrugged and crawled under their blankets. It was going to be a long night.

Dakota settled into Yemaya's home quite nicely. The staff was friendly and accommodating. They obviously enjoyed working for the Lysannes. She spent her mornings walking with Yemaya, then excused herself to work on her article. The castle was isolated but was furnished with all the modern conveniences. Internet connections were accessible by satellite, so she was able to update her boss on her research.

Yemaya spent most of her time catching up on estate matters and helping the local families settle small disputes or resolve problems. Usually, Raidon handled petty quarrels, but she felt he needed a break from his routine so he could spend some time with Reymone. The two took a trip to Cahul to check on rumors of several suspicious men having arrived in Moldova the week before. They were more than happy to mix business with pleasure if it meant getting away for a few days.

When Yemaya was away on business, Dakota took long walks through the forest. She grew used to the noises of the animals and the shadows dancing around as the sun moved across the sky. Still had it not been for Simtire's company, she doubted she could find her way back alone. There was something creepy about the woods, probably due more to Yemaya's stories than anything else.

At breakfast, Yemaya told a story about some sheep that were found in the valley with their throats cut. Everyone was afraid a drac— their word for devil—had returned. It amazed her how much the legend of Dracula dominated the culture. At night, when the wind blew and the wolves howled, the superstitious muttered prayers and crossed themselves. Few ventured into the darkness. Even those employed by the Lysannes rarely traveled after the sun set. When she asked Yemaya why, she shrugged.

"It is hard for some to overcome generations of superstition. Even the most enlightened of us hide within our being ancient fears. We may think we have banished them, but when the sun sets, the winds blow, and things go bump in the night, our hearts still pound. We hold our breaths, trying to make sense of the noises, and we pray what we hear is only overactive imaginations. It is the nature of man to fear. Our species would have died long ago without it."

"I suppose so. Did the authorities ever find out who killed the sheep?"

"Eventually. It turned out to be some kids who belonged to a cult group that worshiped the legend of the count. They were making sacrifices, hoping to resurrect him. I cannot imagine what they thought he would do if they had managed it. Thank them? Vampires are not known for gratitude."

"Thought you didn't believe in them," Dakota teased.

"Like I said, I have no reason to yet. But I never totally discount possibilities."

Dakota sipped her coffee and watched Yemaya as she scanned the local newspaper. After several moments, Yemaya glanced up, giving her a questioning look.

"Go ahead and ask," she offered.

Startled, Dakota blushed.

"Oh, sorry," she apologized. "I was just wondering about something."

"I see. About me, I gather."

"Well, yes...although it's not really important. I'm more curious than anything. I've noticed that you're multilingual. Besides the obvious—English, French, and Romanian—are there any others?"

Yemaya chuckled.

"A few. Why do you ask?"

"No reason. You seem very fluent in the ones I've heard. You have a slight accent when you speak English but nothing distinctive enough to identify your origin. If it weren't for a certain Old World formality, you could almost pass yourself off as an American."

"Old World?"

"Yeah, you know, proper English. I've noticed you never use contractions. I don't believe I've really ever heard someone talk 'long hand,'" Dakota joked.

"I suppose you have a point. My tutor was a very *proper English* woman from the old school. She would tell me only illiterates used lingual shortcuts. Obviously, she was greatly mistaken, but I find myself unable to change old habits." Yemaya laughed.

"More likely unwilling," Dakota teased. "But I wouldn't change a thing. It gives you a certain...um...mystery and suits you. So what are you doing today?" she asked, changing the subject.

"I must drive into town to talk with some of my people. They have requested my presence to resolve some issues."

"Don't you get tired of acting as mediator?"

"Not really. My family has always settled disputes amongst my people. Normally, Raidon would do it, but since he is away, it falls on me. What are you going to do?"

"Mostly work on my article. Probably take a walk later."

"Take Simtire. She likes your company, and she will guide you home should you become lost."

"Seems I have no choice. She's always waiting for me," Dakota joked.

"She is part of you now as you are her. It is the way of wolves. Now remember you must be back by dark. The nights are cold, and Simtire is still too young to be completely reliable once the sun sets. Even wolves grow uneasy at night without their pack. She will want to be with the others."

"No problem. I certainly don't want to be caught out after the sun sets. It's creepy enough during the day."

"I really need to go now. Andrei is waiting with the car."

Dakota walked along with Yemaya to the Hummer. Andrei stood next to the vehicle, holding the door open.

"Good morning, Andrei."

"Good morning, Ms. Devereaux," he acknowledged, smiling broadly.

Yemaya motioned for Andrei to get in the car. Then turning, she stepped close to Dakota, cupping her face between her palms.

"The day will be long without you," she whispered.

Gulping, Dakota nodded.

"I will see you this evening. Then I think the time has come for us to talk," Yemaya murmured as she lowered her lips to Dakota's. The kiss was fleeting but held the promise of much more. Dakota felt her heart racing as the taller woman backed away and climbed into the Hummer. Waving, she watched it disappear down the road.

Robert Chisholm opened the large envelope stamped confidential that had just been delivered to him. Inside was a detailed report on the mountainous region of Romania and Moldova. His researchers managed to put together a rather detailed report on the history of the land and its people.

Scanning the documents, he noticed several references to a small population of locals called Carpi. They were a clannish group having limited contact with the rest of the world. Rarely did they venture far from the homeland, and when they did, it was never for long periods. The report cited several legends connecting them to the legendary Vladmir Dracul. Snorting his disgust, he was about to throw it aside when his eye caught the name Lysanne. Immediately intrigued, he read the entire file.

Raidon Lysanne was considered the leader of the Carpi people. His older sister, Yemaya, seemed to hold an equal status. They were the offspring from a marriage between a French-Canadian named Vincente Lysanne and Anya Lupescu, the only child of Beles and Drenkova Lupescu, former leaders of the clan. Beles Lupescu was killed in a riding accident. Her husband died a few weeks later. Some said of a broken heart.

The report continued on, giving the reported lineage of the Lupescu family back to the fourteenth century. The exact origin of the name was unknown, but it meant "son of wolf." The Lupescu's rule over the Carpi remained uninterrupted as far back as the researchers could tell.

Leaning back in his chair, Chisholm stared out the window. So Ms. Lysanne was some form of royalty. *Interesting.* Chisholm continued to scan the report. The last paragraph particularly interested him. It stated legends attributed some of the Carpi people, and especially their leaders, with unique powers like the ability to "influence" those around them. Although Chisholm wasn't quite sure what was meant by "influence," the fact it was highlighted was enough to tell him he needed to meet Yemaya Lysanne.

This might explain how she pulled off her illusions so well and why cameras and electronic equipment were never allowed during her performances. She could fool the people, but it would be more difficult to fool electronics. Picking up his phone, he dialed Jones's cell number. After several rings, a voice answered.

"Eddy Jones here."

"Jones, what's happening over there?" Chisholm demanded.

"At the moment, we're hiking through this god awful forest trying to get to the Lysanne place before sunset. No one said we'd be playing Boy Scout in the woods," Eddy grumbled.

"I'm not interested in your personal problems, Jones. When you find out something more definite, call me. I want this woman caught and brought back to me unharmed. Do you understand?"

"Yeah, boss. It may not be easy, though. Seems she's popular around here. Trying to smuggle her out of this country is going to take a lot of dollars."

"I don't care how much it costs. I want her at my country home within two weeks. Do you understand?"

"Sure, boss. Two weeks. I'll call you once we have her."

"Good. And, Jones, remember she doesn't show up, don't you show up," Chisholm threatened.

"Uh...no problem. We'll get her."

Slamming the phone down, Chisholm folded the report and leaned back in his chair. He had sensed there was more to this woman than just smoke and mirrors. Now he was sure. Somehow, she was controlling the audience. If he could figure out how, he could use it to his own advantage.

"Shit," he smirked. "I could be president."

Laughing at the thought, Chisholm left for a board meeting, his mind already visualizing how he would make the bastards kiss his ass once he took control.

Eddy flipped the phone cover shut and swore.

"Someone ought to shoot that fuckin' bastard," he grumbled.

"What's up, Eddy?" Jimmy asked.

"Nothing. Chisholm just wants us to speed things up. Says he wants that broad back in Miami in two weeks. He has no concept of what it's gonna take to snatch her, then smuggle the woman across the border without getting caught. Asshole thinks money solves everything."

"Well, it seems to have for him. He calls the shots and we jump," Jimmy grumbled.

"Yeah, and if we don't jump this time and succeed, we're all going to be living out the rest of our lives in this stinkin' little country. How much farther, Kerc?"

Shrugging, Kerc pointed to the next ridge.

"Maybe two hour. Maybe less. We climb there. Then you see *castel fort.*"

Two hours later, the five men lay on a precipice overlooking Yemaya's home. With binoculars, they checked for a weakness in the building or landscaping but found nothing useful.

"Shit. It's a fuckin' fort," Billy groaned.

"Yeah. How are we supposed to get someone out of there?" Jimmy asked.

"Just keep watching. Something might come up," Eddy said.

As if conjuring up a solution, they saw Yemaya and a young woman walking toward a Hummer that had just pulled up to the drawbridge. The intimate kiss between the two women took them by surprise.

"Jesus fuckin' Christ," Jimmy cursed. "They're dykes."

"What a waste of good pussy," Billy said. "I bet I could change their minds."

"You couldn't change a piss ant's mind, you cocksucker," Jimmy sneered.

"And you think you could? Last time you had a woman, you had to get her so drunk she didn't know what she was doing, and even then, you had to tie her down to spread her legs. At least my women come willingly," Jimmy smirked.

"You two, shut up," Eddy ordered disgustedly. "You ain't doing nothing to no one. Chisholm wants the woman untouched. You understand that? That means you keep your dicks in your pants and your hands in your pockets until she's delivered."

"Yeah, well, nothing says we can't have some fun with the other one, now does it?" Billy asked.

Shaking his head, Eddy went back to watching. When the car drove off, he slipped back down the hill.

"You two keep an eye out. Maybe we can use the other woman for bait if the opportunity arises. I'm gonna scout around."

Chapter Ten

Dakota threw down her pen in frustration. Why was it every time she started writing about Yemaya, her pens ran out of ink?

"They're cursed," she mumbled. "How can you curse a friggin' pen?"

Looking around Yemaya's desk for something else, she found several pencils.

"A-ha!" she whooped. "This will do." Ecstatic, she began scribbling.

Snick! The lead tip snapped. Picking up another pencil, she tried again.

Snick!

Cursing, she threw the pencil against the wall in frustration.

"That's it. I'm done."

How was she going to write about Yemaya if she couldn't get anything to work? Rocking back on two chair legs, she crossed her arms and stared out the window. Worried about disclosing too much about Yemaya, she needed to think about her article a little more.

She still didn't understand how the woman pulled off her illusions. For sure, she couldn't disclose the information about her people's ability to influence or control others. Talk about creating mass hysteria. Just the thought of being controlled by another was frightening enough. If it was true, the Carpis would be hunted down and slaughtered—or worse, captured and made into guinea pigs. Who wouldn't want to possess such power? Few would use it wisely.

Sighing, she realized she needed some help from Yemaya in explaining her illusions, something that would satisfy the readers but not give away valuable information that could jeopardize her people.

I guess there's nothing for me to do but wait for Yemaya's return, Dakota thought, glaring at the offending tools of her trade. Picking up her pen, she shook it in exasperation.

"You'd better not work for her or I'm tossing you for good," she warned. "Well, it's as good a time as any for a walk."

Dakota grabbed her jacket and told the housekeeper she was taking a stroll through the woods.

"You must be back before dark, Ms. Dakota," Maria cautioned. "Ms. Yemaya will be very upset if you are not here when she arrives."

Patting the older woman on the shoulder, Dakota assured her she had no intention of staying out past sunset. Losing her way in the forest was not her idea of a good time.

Halfway across the drawbridge, Simtire was sitting patiently, her wolfish grin giving her a goofy look. Dakota ruffled the thick fur of the silver wolf and motioned her to go on. Eagerly, Simtire ran off toward the path leading to Dakota's favorite spot, a small cluster of boulders overlooking the river. She had discovered it several days earlier and enjoyed the shelter from the cool breezes as she watched the sun move slowly across the sky.

Jimmy watched the woman and large dog walking toward the woods.

"Hey, Eddy. Get over here," he yelled.

"What's up?"

"Looks like the big dyke's girlfriend is taking a walk. This might be the best chance at grabbing her. Once we get her, we can get the other bitch to do anything."

"Maybe. Let's see if we can catch up with her." Turning to the guide, he asked if he knew where she might be going.

"Is possible she go there," he replied pointing to some large boulders several hundred feet up. "Good view."

"Get us there first."

Kerc nodded.

Dakota climbed the steep incline to the huge boulders. Simtire wandered around, stopping occasionally to sniff at a rock or plant. In one spot, she turned her back to Dakota, squatting to pee.

"That's ladylike," Dakota laughed.

As if understanding her remark, Simtire gave her an indignant look and stalked away.

"Sorry," Dakota yelled, shaking her head in amusement. "Sheesh! Who'd have guessed you were so sensitive?"

Several yards in front of her, she noticed the wolf stop abruptly, her hackles raised. Head lowered, a deep growl rumbled from her throat, her lips curling upward, revealing long white canines. Looking in the direction the wolf was staring, she watched several men step from behind the trees and walk toward her. Backing away, Dakota was halted by a large boulder. Simtire moved quickly to stand in front of her.

"Hey, fellas. What's up?" she asked nervously, her right hand grasping Simtire's neck fur.

"You are," Jimmy smirked. "Come along nicely and just maybe we won't hurt you."

Simtire crouched ready to launch herself at anyone within reach of Dakota.

"I'm not going anywhere. What do you want?" Dakota demanded, her voice trembling.

"Like I said, bitch, you."

Dakota recognized the lust in the larger man's eyes. Maybe the others wouldn't touch her, but this one definitely had rape in mind.

"Shut up, Jimmy," Eddy ordered. "Look, miss. You have to come with us. Do it peacefully and no one gets hurt. We aren't looking for any trouble here."

"Well, I don't know you, and I sure as hell am not going anywhere with you. You're trespassing. If I'm not home shortly, they'll come looking for me," Dakota bluffed.

"Guess we'd better get a move on it then," Eddy replied, motioning for the others to take her.

Simtire launched herself at Billy, fangs ripping through the skin and muscles of his arm. Screaming, her momentum and weight pushed him off balance, causing him to fall. Jimmy and Chuck tried to pull the wolf off Billy.

Simtire spun around, snapping viciously at anyone within range of her teeth. Billy screamed again as blood poured from the open gashes. Distracted from her first victim, Simtire lunged at Chuck, massive jaws clamping down on his thigh, severing muscles and vessels. Cursing, he beat at the wolf frantically with clenched fists.

Dakota stood transfixed, watching Simtire's gallant efforts to defend her. She didn't notice Jimmy pulling out a pistol and pointing it. It wasn't until she heard the gunfire and saw Simtire collapse that she realized the young wolf had been shot. As Chuck pushed the limp body away, he grabbed his leg, moaning loudly.

The winds died, and the forest became eerily quiet. The howling of wolves invaded the silence, causing the men to glance around nervously.

"Goddamn it. Get me a tourniquet or something. I'm gonna bleed to death," Chuck yelled, trying to stop the flow of blood. Eddy motioned his guide to help the wounded men. Surprisingly, Kerc backed away in horror, his right hand crossing his chest to ward off evil spirits.

"You kill the lup...you bring the drac down on us. I no help. I no stay. My family cursed," the guide yelled before disappearing into the woods.

"You," Eddy ordered, turning to Dakota. "Get over here and help them."

"Fuck you. I'm not helping anyone," Dakota screamed, tears streaming down her cheeks as she stared at Simtire's still body.

Jimmy walked toward her, pointing the gun at her chest.

"Listen, bitch. You do as Eddy says or I'll kill you, too," he hissed.

Dakota began inching along the boulder toward the precipice. With any luck, she might be able to jump onto a ledge about twenty-five feet below. She had noticed it when she and Yemaya had visited the site earlier.

"Jimmy, put the gun away," Eddy snapped. "Give me a hand with these two, and we'll deal with her later."

"I'm dealing with her now. She's gonna be nice and do as I say or I'll teach her a lesson she'll never forget," Jimmy threatened, grabbing his crotch suggestively.

"I said take care of those two. I'll deal with her." Eddy turned toward Dakota. "Look, lady, I suggest you just do what I say and no one gets hurt."

Jimmy sneered, deciding to obey Eddy's order but not before puckering his lips in a pretend kiss. Dakota had no doubts as to what would happen if he ever got his hands on her. She continued moving toward the edge of the cliff, making sure to keep distance between her and the others.

"I know you," she said angrily, making eye contact with Eddy. "You're the one taking pictures at Yemaya's shows. You've been stalking her. Why?"

"Now, lady, don't do nothing stupid. My boss just wants to talk to her about something."

Eddy began to sweat profusely. It wasn't hard to figure out what she was thinking. He dared not approach her too quickly. If she fell or jumped, he'd have nothing to bargain with.

"So why go to all this trouble just to talk? Why not just call her and set up an appointment?" she asked, her eyes darting toward the cliff's edge.

The howling of wolves grew closer, making the men extremely nervous.

"Come on, Eddy. Grab the broad and let's get out of here. I don't like the sound of those wolves. They seem to be getting closer," Jimmy yelled.

Eddy decided he couldn't wait any longer. Lunging toward Dakota, he grabbed at her arm. Dakota anticipated his move and stepped backward, feeling nothing but air under her foot. Eddy barely managed to grab her coat sleeve before it was ripped from his hand. All he saw was the woman's face, her eyes wide with fear, as she fell—and something else. Instead of surprise like he had seen on Brenda Simpson's face, he saw the resolute expression of a person determined not to be captured. For a split second, he actually felt sad, an emotion long forgotten.

Standing on the edge of the cliff, he looked down. The woman's body lay about twenty feet below. She didn't move. Not having any rope, he decided they needed to leave quickly and find their way back to the van. Hopefully, the guide would wait for them, although he doubted it.

"Okay, fellas, let's get out of here before someone comes looking for her."

He and Jimmy helped Chuck to his feet. Billy clutched his arm against his side, cursing vehemently.

The howling grew louder, causing the group to hurry down the trail in the direction they had come.

The last thing Dakota remembered was falling and a sharp pain before losing consciousness. She awoke to the smell of wood smoke, chanting, and the feel of a hand stroking her hair.

"Oh, shit," she moaned, wincing as she touched a large bump on the back of her head.

Opening her eyes, she found herself lying on a blanket next to a warm, flickering campfire. Grandma Dakota sat next to her.

"What happened, Grandma?" Dakota whispered, the pain easing slightly.

"Hush, chile. Ya 'bout killed yerself is what happened, but ya be safe now."

"Am I dead?"

"Nah. Ifn ya was daid, ya'd not be lying here by a warm farh. Ya'd be at them purly gates beatin' on the doors," Grandma Dakota teased. "Ya jest be hidin' in the spirit world for now. Only way ta keep ya safe till the magic woman come fer ya."

"Those men. They killed Simtire," she cried, tears streaming down her cheeks.

"Now, now, chile, the spirits looks after their own. That young pup is tough. If it be her time, then she died defendin' someone she loved. No better way ta go than thet, now is thar?"

"I guess so, Grandma, but I feel guilty. I should've sent her away."

"Ya couldn't haf sent her away any more than she coulda you. Seems ya tried to do the same as her by jumpin' off that thar mountain."

"That's different. Those men were after Yemaya. They meant to hurt her, I'm sure."

"That be the truth, youngun, but I sees no diffrence in the wolfling givin' her life for ya and ya givin' yers for the magic woman. It all be for love."

"I never really thought I had a choice. I'd do it again if I had to."

Smiling, Grandma Dakota continued stroking her granddaughter's hair.

"I knowed, chile. That thar's the way it bes. Now ya just lies here and rest. She be on her way ta gets ya. Won't be long now."

Feeling warm and drowsy, Dakota closed her eyes.

"Grandma?" she whispered.

"Yes, chile, what is it?"

"I love you," Dakota replied sleepily.

"I luvs ya, too, chile."

Once Dakota was asleep, the elder Dakota raised her right arm to eye level, bending it at the elbow. The flames from the fire began to waver from a breeze caused by beating wings. A small brown hawk settled gently on the extended arm, its talons wrapping around her forearm.

"Ya needs to seek out the magic woman, Ladyhawk. If she don't finds my grandchile and the wolfpup this night, theys be gonners fer shore. Now skeedaddle. We doesn't have much time."

The hawk screeched when Dakota flipped her arm upward, sending the small bird on her mission.

Yemaya had just settled a dispute with three local business owners when she felt a strange uneasiness. Shaking her head, she tried to dispel a feeling that something was horribly wrong. The urge to get home was strong, almost to the point of physical pain. Calling Andrei to bring the Hummer, she jumped in and dialed the estate.

"Lysanne residence," Maria answered.

"Maria, may I speak with Ms. Devereaux?"

"She's not here, mistress. She went for a walk hours ago and hasn't returned," Maria replied nervously. "I have sent the men to look for her. The wolves, there are so many of them now, and they howl continuously. I fear something terrible has happened."

"I am on my way. I will be there as quickly as possible. Call me if she shows up."

Yemaya hung up the phone and turned to her driver.

"Andrei, hurry. Something's wrong. Maria said the wolves are on the move."

Nodding, he floored the accelerator. If the wolves were involved, something was definitely amiss. Twenty minutes later, Yemaya was charging up the hillside toward the ridge Dakota and she visited. Several men followed closely behind. The wolf pack ran in front. When the party reached the open area, the wolves stopped abruptly, heads lowered and hackles raised. Slowly, they approached the body of Simtire, sniffing and nudging her with their noses.

Regina lay next to her, her head resting on the body of her daughter, whining softly. Voinic, unable to console his life mate, sat a few feet away with the rest of the pack. Yemaya walked over to Simtire and knelt, feeling for signs of life.

"Regina, a departa," Yemaya ordered. Reluctantly, Regina stood and moved away, lying next to her mate.

"Bohria, a tutel, Simtire, degraba," Yemaya said to one of the men.

"Da, maestra." Gently picking up the limp body as if it were a fragile child, the burly man moved rapidly down the path toward home. Regina nosed Tanc and Clovn. Growling softly, she looked at the man walking away with her daughter's body. The two siblings stood and loped after Bohria. Standing, Regina walked to the edge of the cliff, followed closely by Voinic. Sniffing the air, they peered into the darkness, eyes focused on Dakota's prone form several feet below.

Their whine brought an immediate response from Yemaya and the men. She ordered them to tie a rope around a tree. Then tying it around her waist, she was lowered onto the ledge. Once she was assured it would hold her weight, she untied the rope and shifted her position so she could examine Dakota.

Her heartbeat and breathing seemed okay. Running her hands slowly up and down Dakota's body, the only serious injury seemed to be the large bump on the back of her head. She would be sore for a few days, but nothing seemed broken or sprained. Breathing a sigh of relief, Yemaya told the men to lower another rope. Tying it securely around Dakota and the other around herself, she instructed them to pull them up slowly. Once on top, she slipped her arms under Dakota and stood, not saying a word. The men and the wolves followed silently behind.

At the drawbridge, Yemaya turned to Regina and Voinic. The two wolves sensed the controlled anger of their mistress and growled in empathy. One of their pups had also been hurt by the humans. Revenge would taste sweet.

"No, you know what to do. Do not let any strangers leave the forest until I find out who did this, but you will not hurt them. I must know more about this."

Disappointed, the two wolves pointed their noses skyward and howled. Tanc and Clovn joined in. The four turned and loped into the woods, the scent of the men fresh in their nostrils. At least the hunt would be fun. Once they found their prey, they would obey their mistress, but she hadn't forbidden them from tormenting the humans.

Yemaya took Dakota to her bed, telling Maria to bring warm water and bandages. When she began washing away the blood, the injured woman groaned, her hand reaching to feel the bump.

"Shh," Yemaya whispered, stopping the hand before it touched the wound. "Everything is okay. Go to sleep, love."

Opening one eye, Dakota stared blankly at Yemaya, not sure if she was awake or dreaming.

"Grandma? What happened?" she asked groggily.

"I am not your grandma, Dakota. It is Yemaya. You had an accident. You fell and hit your head."

Frowning, Dakota tried to remember the fall. When she did, she tried to sit up, only to be pushed back down.

"Those men, they shot Simtire," Dakota cried frantically. "You have to get her."

"Lie still, Dakota. We have Simtire. Andrei is taking care of her."

Nodding, Dakota settled back onto the bed.

"She tried to protect me, but there were too many. Is she okay? Is she going to die?"

"In time, sweetie, but not this night, I promise. She will have to take it easy for a while. Now what about these men? Who were they?"

"I don't know. One was that man with the camera. He called one Jimmy and one Billy. Simtire injured two of them before Jimmy shot her. I thought he had killed her, then I recognized the guy from your show. His name is Eddy. I knew he was going to use me to get to you, and I couldn't chance it, so..."

Dakota didn't finish the sentence.

"So you decided to sacrifice yourself for me, eh?" Yemaya asked, stunned at the woman's courage.

"Well, I wouldn't say that. I knew there was a ledge below, and I thought I might be able to land on it. I didn't count on hitting my head so hard, though," she joked, then winced.

"Or that the ledge might give way from your weight when you landed, I suppose," Yemaya added, frowning at the image.

"Oh...uh...no...I didn't even think about that," Dakota said sheepishly.

"We can discuss this another time. For now, you need to sleep. If you need anything, I will be right here."

"You don't mean you're going to spend the night in that chair. It doesn't look very comfortable. If you're gonna be my nursemaid, at least lie here next to me and keep me warm," Dakota pleaded. "I feel cold, Yemaya." As if to prove it, she shivered.

"A little bit of exposure, I think, but how could I refuse sleeping next to a beautiful woman?" Yemaya teased.

Slipping out of her pants and blouse, she climbed into bed, wrapping her arms around the smaller woman and drawing her close. Her body heat quickly warmed the injured woman, causing her sore muscles to relax. Within minutes, Dakota was asleep. Only then did Yemaya feel it was safe to drift off herself. It was a miracle Dakota landed on the ledge, let alone suffered such minor injuries.

Chapter Eleven

Instead of stumbling through the darkness, the five men decided to pitch camp for the night. Not wanting to attract attention, they thought it better not to start a fire. Chuck's leg was badly swollen. Infection was setting in, and Billy's arm was in a similar condition. If they didn't get treated within the next few days, both men would be in danger of losing a limb or dying.

"This is just fuckin' great," Jimmy complained. "Lost in the woods with two cripples and our one chance at getting the woman gone."

"I'm sick of your complaints, Jimmy. Just shut up and help clean those wounds before they get any more infected," Eddy snapped.

"I'm no fuckin' nursemaid. You help them."

Grabbing his blanket, Jimmy lay down by a tree, leaving the others to take care of themselves. Closing his eyes, he was almost asleep when he heard a growl. Glancing around, he noticed several pairs of glowing red eyes staring at him and the others.

"Eddy," he yelled nervously. "There are wolves out there."

"Shut up, Jimmy. They won't bother us if we don't bother them. Just don't make any sudden moves."

Watching the wolves, Jimmy pulled his gun out and pointed it at the spot he had seen the eyes. Nothing was there. A growl to his left made him turn quickly in the other direction. Red eyes glowed ominously.

"Bullshit. They attacked Billy and Chuck. They sure as hell will attack us."

Frightened, he fired at the spot he last saw the eyes. Again they had disappeared.

"Damn it, Jimmy," Eddy screamed, walking over to grab the gun. "I said they won't bother us, but they sure as hell will if you threaten them. They're probably just curious about us. Now if you aren't going to help, shut the fuck up and go to sleep."

Picking up his blanket, Jimmy moved closer to the three men. If he was going to get attacked, he damn well wanted them there with him.

Dakota drank in the warmth of the body lying next to her. The feel of muscular arms wrapped protectively around her and the warm body pressed against her back felt wonderful. Turning her head slowly, she looked at the sleeping woman. Black hair partially hid Yemaya's face before spreading across the pillow, across her shoulders, and down her chest. Her skin was a golden brown, more natural than tanned.

"You are so beautiful," she whispered, reaching out to brush her fingers lightly down the sleeping woman's exposed arm. "How can I compete with anyone for someone like you?"

Blue eyes opened slowly, trapping her gaze.

"There is no one else," Yemaya answered softly, her warm breath fanning Dakota's cheek. "Surely you know that by now."

"I hoped. I prayed. Even Grandma Dakota hinted a few times, but I never really believed I could have you," she whispered back.

"Well, listen to Grandma Dakota. She seems to know an awful lot," Yemaya teased.

"From now on, I will."

"How are you feeling?" Yemaya asked, reaching over to touch the lump on Dakota's head.

"Actually, pretty good. Warm, relaxed," Dakota answered, brushing the hair away from the other woman's eyes.

"Good. You hungry?"

Images of Yemaya naked in bed with her made her blush. Yemaya laughed.

"Guess you *are* feeling better," she chuckled. Pushing up on one elbow, she leaned forward and kissed Dakota, her lips lingering. Backing off, she stared into her eyes, her own passion growing.

"I do not think you are up to this yet," Yemaya said, her voice husky with desire.

"Don't think then. I've been ready for this all my life," Dakota whispered softy.

Dakota wrapped her arms around Yemaya's neck, pulling her head back down.

"Love me, Yemaya," Dakota begged, her breathing ragged.

Yemaya flashed her a huge grin. Needing no further encouragement, she pushed the sheets away and stared hungrily at Dakota. Undoing the buttons, she gently opened Dakota's shirt and gazed at her erect nipples. Yemaya felt a rush of heat. She felt Dakota tremble against her palms as she cupped warm round breasts. Leaning down, she kissed each one reverently.

"You are so beautiful," she said, her voice husky with desire.

Dakota ran her fingers through Yemaya's hair, then stroked her cheek. Touching another woman had never been so intoxicating. Their kiss became hot as Yemaya's hand circled Dakota's ribs. Yemaya pushed the shirt from Dakota's shoulders, tugging it away and tossing it on the floor. Dakota groaned when Yemaya ran her thumb across the hardened nipples, palms pressed warmly against her breast. She kneaded each one gently.

Dakota stiffened in anticipation when she felt Yemaya's hand slip from her breast and move downward across her abdomen toward her thighs. Arching her back, she inhaled deeply, trying to control her anticipation.

"What do you want?" Yemaya whispered.

Dakota could only groan. Smiling, Yemaya began stroking Dakota's inner thigh. "You like this?" she asked playfully.

"Uh-huh" was all Dakota could say, her body craving more.

Yemaya was eager to oblige. Dakota felt the fires of passion rage when Yemaya's fingers wandered between her legs. As the taller woman slid her own body down, she lowered her head, pressing her lips to Dakota's sex. Her silky tongue parted Dakota's lips, dipping slowly in to taste the warm liquid.

Dakota gasped when she felt the hot, wet muscle caress her vulva, barely touching her clit as it sampled the salty sweetness. She grasped Yemaya's hair, pressing her head downward as spasms racked her body. She groaned loudly, arching her back, her breathing coming in short gasps.

"Oh, fuck. You're killing me," she groaned loudly. She had never felt this fire before.

"No, love, I could never stand the loss," Yemaya replied, straightening up to kiss Dakota.

Seeing the need in Dakota's eyes, she decided to end her lover's misery. Yemaya shifted, easing her fingers between Dakota's legs. Trailing them back and forth across the soft skin, she leaned down and inhaled deeply. Lying on her side, she pulled the woman's hips toward her. Separating the skin with her thumb and finger, she bent forward. A warm musky scent drifted tantalizingly toward her.

Lowering her head, she slowly stroked the vulva, tasting the salty liquid. Dakota pushed her hips upward, and

Yemaya pressed her mouth tightly against the moist lips and caressed the area with her tongue. Moving it slowly at first, she alternated between long, slow strokes and short, rapid ones.

Dakota's hips moved to the beat of Yemaya's tongue. It was becoming impossible to hold the younger woman down, so Yemaya circled her arms around Dakota's legs and raised her hips in the air, the woman's thighs rested on her shoulders. Plunging her hard tongue into the slick opening, she began pumping it in and out, then swirling it around while her right thumb flicked back and forth across the swollen clit.

Dakota's legs trembled from the strain of pushing upward in an effort to increase the pleasure. Just when she was about to collapse, she felt her body lifted, arms wrapped tightly around her thighs, and a hard tongue enter her vagina. The feeling was incredible. Muscles tensed, at first from a tingling, then from the indescribable sensations coursing through her body.

Yemaya's lips circled her clit and sucked gently, her tongue firmly stroking the soft skin. Unable to control herself, Dakota screamed Yemaya's name and collapsed from the strain. Yemaya gently lowered Dakota's hips to the sheets. Gathering the exhausted woman in her arms, she pressed her lover's head into her shoulder.

"Shh...Sleep, baby," she whispered.

Dakota felt the words drift slowly through her mind and remembered the first time she had heard Yemaya speak. She thought her voice was seductive then. She knew its power now. Smiling, she nestled into the firm shoulder beneath her cheek. Both drifted into a peaceful slumber.

"So, ya finally gots a taste of honey, eh?" Grandma Dakota chuckled.

Yemaya did *not* want to open her eyes nor did she want to have this type of conversation with Dakota's grandmother.

"Now don't ya go pretendin' ya don't hear me," the older woman admonished. "I knowed ya feelin' all warm and comfertables, but we needs to jaw a bit."

Sighing, Yemaya opened one eye and looked at the woman.

"Could you at least wait a while? I am tired," Yemaya groaned, closing her eye.

"Ifn I could wait, chile, I woulda. Taint like me ta go bargin' in where I ain't wanted."

"So you say," Yemaya grumbled. Opening both eyes, she noticed she was still in the meadow. "What can I do for you, Grandma Dakota?"

"I sees ya thinks of me as family now."

"If you are Dakota's family, you are mine, too," Yemaya smirked. "There is no need to tell you how I feel about Dakota. You know my thoughts."

"That be the truth, magic woman. Ifn ya felt tutherwise, ya wouldn't be a tastin' that sweet honey cuz I'd be puttin' the roots on ya."

"I bet you would, too," Yemaya agreed, laughing. "I imagine you know how Dakota feels also."

"Yep. I shore nuff do. Likes I said, ya wouldn't be a tastin' the honey ifn either of ya twernt a carin' deeply for tother. But nuff of this. Them chilins of yourn has sniffed out them thar troublemakers. Ifn ya don't want them doin' no harm ta them thar rascals, ya needs to get a movin'. The spirits be keepin' the wolves calmed, but they be a wantin' to avenge the wolf pup. Only ya can makes them mind now so ya best hurry up."

"I guess you are right, Granny. I need to find out what this is all about."

Grandma Dakota smiled at Yemaya's unconscious acceptance of her as family.

"Ya knowed in yoh heart what this bes 'bout, chile. Pawer. There bes a man who wants yoh pawer, and he's a willin' ta kill for it. Ifn he finds the truth 'bout you and yourn, yoh people will be hunted and used to make him more pawerful. Ya needs to do what ya needs to do to make shore he don't get that thar knowledge."

"I know. I guess I should get moving." Leaning toward the older woman, Yemaya kissed her cheek. "Thanks, Granny, and thanks for having such a wonderful great-great-granddaughter."

Patting her knee, Grandma Dakota chuckled.

"Yoh welcome, chile. Ya has waited a long time for someone good nuff for ya. I'm happy for the two of yas."

The four men couldn't get any rest. The wolves made sure of it. Being hunters, they knew tired prey made mistakes. Prowling the darkness, they growled or snarled loudly whenever someone fell asleep. By sunrise, everyone was so irritable, the group just packed up and left without eating, hoping to be headed in the right direction. Occasionally, the men would spot furtive movements in the shadows and veer off in an effort to avoid the wolves. Little did they know they were being herded in a circle.

Voinic was getting restless. As the alpha male, he wanted to avenge Simtire. Only the death of her attackers would satisfy his thirst, and only the will of his mistress kept him from exacting revenge. His patience was limited, though. Sensing her mate's thoughts, Regina walked to him, touching her nose to his. She too wanted vengeance, but their mistress wished otherwise. She would not permit her pack to violate the trust the Carpi placed in them.

The wolves of these mountain ranges had been companions to the Lupescu family for hundreds of years. The alliance benefited both Carpi and wolf. Their lives were forever intertwined and their loyalty was absolute.

"We're fuckin' lost."

"Damn it, Jimmy. Shut the fuck up," Billy yelled, annoyed at having to listen to the other man's whining. "You're always bitchin' about something."

"Fuck you, Billy. We're lost and you're too stupid to realize it. Those wolves have been controlling us, and no one here seems to have noticed."

"I noticed," Eddy said. "I don't know what you think we're suppose to do about it. You shot that wolf. I hear wolves are intelligent and very protective of their own. I told you that gun would get us in trouble."

"At least I kept that wolf from killing us. It's more than what you did. And I don't care if these things are Einsteins. I ain't lettin' no wolf control me," Jimmy snarled.

"And just what are you going to do about it, Jimmy? We have one gun. Shit, we don't even know how many wolves are out there. I suppose we could try killing the ones we see, but what if there's more than five? Then what? Right now they're playing with us. Maybe they'll grow tired and leave, but for sure, I'm not going to piss them off. I suggest you follow suit," Eddy advised.

"All I've got to say is I'm not going to spend another night in this fuckin' place. If it takes killing them all, I'll do it. Even if I have to use my bare hands."

Eddy snorted in disgust. Jimmy was known for his bravado, not his brains. Problem was he never followed through. He was all talk and no action unless the odds were in his favor. Then he was *really* brave.

Yemaya slipped from under the sheets, kissing the sleeping woman on the cheek. Dakota needed rest to heal from her injuries. The extracurricular activities probably hadn't helped either.

Well, maybe they did, Yemaya thought smugly. *They certainly helped me.*

Before leaving, she gave instructions to Maria about caring for Dakota. A small pack was strapped to her back. Inside was enough gear for one night in case she couldn't make it back by sunset. At the foot of the drawbridge stood Balba, a large black wolf from across the ridge. A younger gray wolf sat slightly behind him. Balba was one of Regina's older siblings but now had his own family. Verdina, his mate, was hidden deep within their den. She was pregnant and due to give birth shortly.

"Hello, Balba." Yemaya knelt, letting the wolf lick her face. "Thank you for coming, but you must go to Verdina. She will need your protection."

The wolf lowered his head, growling unhappily. He and Verdina knew about Simtire. He was aware of Regina and her pack's movements and where they were. It was his duty to help.

"You have a duty to protect your life mate, Balba. Go home. Young Shina here will take me to the men who did this. It will be a good lesson for her."

Reluctantly, Balba turned and trotted into the woods. It would be good to be with Verdina. This was their first time bearing pups and both were worried.

"Well, Shina, shall we go?"

The young gray wolf grinned happily. She loved being near the mistress.

Three hours later, Shina stopped. Raising her nose to the sky, she howled loudly. Within minutes, Regina and Voinic appeared. Seeing Yemaya, they ran to her, nuzzling her hand.

"Simtire is fine. She will be sore and needs rest," Yemaya explained.

Both wolves raised their faces to the sky and howled joyfully. Their howls were greeted by others until the mountains reverberated with the sounds and echoes of the distant packs.

"Where are they?" Yemaya demanded, interrupting the chorus. It was time to find out why the men were following her.

FRAN HECKROTTE

Chapter Twelve

Chuck rested against a log, unable to move his leg. Billy's arm was swollen, red streaks running up the forearm and bicep. He was sweating from the fever caused by the infection. Eddy walked around restlessly, unsure of his next move. The wolves were playing with them, but to what purpose?

If Jimmy hadn't been so hasty with the gun and so crude with the woman, he might have talked her into coming with them peacefully. He was sure the wolf would have done whatever she wanted. Now he had to think of something to tell Chisholm. The man would carry out his threats. Maybe he'd just disappear and not tell Chisholm anything. The others could do whatever they wanted—that is, if they made it out of the forest. Right now he wasn't so sure they would. Hearing footsteps, he stopped pacing.

"Eddy," Jimmy said, looking at the others to make sure they couldn't hear him. "I think we need to leave them and try to get help."

"You do, eh? And if we get out of here, how are we gonna find them again?"

"Well, it shouldn't be any problem for the locals. I'm sure they know these woods inside and out."

"And what are we going to tell them? We were going for a stroll and got attacked by wolves?" Eddy's voice dripped with sarcasm.

"We don't have to tell them anything. Just that Billy and Chuck are lost. By the time they're found, we'll be gone."

"I see. And what will Chisholm have to say about leaving them behind?"

"Hmmm...Good point. Maybe we should just kill them. By the time their bodies are found—if they're found—we can come up with something to satisfy Chisholm."

"You gonna do them, Jimmy?" Eddy asked.

"Sure. I don't have any problems eliminating liabilities. I've done it before, and I'll probably have to do it again," Jimmy smirked, proud of himself.

"Am I a liability?"

"Huh?"

"I asked...am I a liability?" Eddy snapped.

"No, of course not. Nothing's wrong with you," Jimmy replied, not realizing his answer said more than he intended.

"Let me think about it for a few minutes. I'll let you know."

Jimmy strolled away, his hands in his pockets, confident Eddy would see he was right. Eddy, on the other hand, was even more worried now. Not knowing what the wolves wanted and whether the girl's body had been discovered was bad enough. He actually felt sorry about her. It took a lot of courage to do what she had done. Eddy respected real courage. Now he had Jimmy to watch.

Billy and Chuck couldn't defend themselves against the large burly man. Reaching into his pocket, he pulled out the gun. Eddy didn't like guns. They caused more trouble than they were worth.

He was thinking about the weapon when he heard a wolf howl. Seconds later, another wolf joined in, then the entire mountain range echoed with the noise. It was frightening to realize how many animals might be out there. For a second, he considered Jimmy's offer to kill the others and run. For a minute, but it wasn't his style. It was one thing to take care of a problem if his boss ordered him to. It was another to kill a partner. Eddy had a peculiar sense of honor.

Yemaya listened to the conversation between Jimmy and Eddy, disgusted at how easily Jimmy was willing to kill. Eddy, though, was different. She sensed he was a killer, but there was a reluctance in him to kill his companions. It wouldn't change his fate, but it did make her sad in a strange way. She wondered what had happened in his life to change him into the person he was. At some point, he must have been a decent man.

Shrugging to herself, she ordered the wolves to surround the group but to keep a safe distance. If Eddy chose to shoot, several of them could be wounded or killed. The two injured men wouldn't be a problem. She suspected Jimmy was the greatest threat. Eddy was a mystery, which made him unpredictable, but he wasn't a loose cannon.

Yemaya decided it was time to make her presence known. She could see Regina and the other wolves moving stealthily through the trees, taking up their positions.

Billy, shivering from the fever, blinked as a woman appeared near Eddy. Shaking his head and mumbling incoherently, he pointed at her. Eddy and Jimmy looked at Billy, then in the direction he was pointing. Eddy jumped when he saw Yemaya only a few feet away. Pointing the gun at her, he backed up.

"I would not even think about it if I were you," Yemaya advised, her voice velvet-covered steel—silky smooth, pleasing to the ear, and determined.

"How'd you get here?" Eddy stammered, glancing around for signs of other people.

Looking past him at Jimmy, Yemaya nodded in his direction.

"Tell your friend to stay where he's at."

Eddy felt compelled to obey her quiet order.

"Stand still, Jimmy. Let me talk to her."

"No problem, Eddy."

Jimmy was as startled as the rest. He had noticed several wolves lying nearby. The previous howling was a warning that there were more wolves concealed by the darkness. The thought of all those teeth tearing into his flesh sickened him.

"Good. You are Eddy." It was a statement, not a question.

He nodded but didn't say anything. Her voice was low, even seductive. It drifted through the air like a warm breeze, soft, soothing, irresistible. Eddy waited for her to speak again, his mind craving the verbal contact.

"Give me the gun, Eddy."

Eddy looked down at the handgun. He had forgotten he still held it. Looking at her, he seemed confused. He knew he needed the gun for something but couldn't remember what. Her voice, her eyes made resistance futile. Still he tried.

"It is okay, Eddy. You never liked guns, remember. Give it to me before someone else gets hurt. Enough have been hurt already. The girl and the wolf will live. You do not want anyone else getting hurt, do you? Now give me the gun."

Eddy could feel his mind surrendering to the compulsion. He stretched out his hand, offering her the weapon. When Jimmy saw Eddy give her the gun, he shouted angrily.

"What the fuck are you doing, Eddy? You just gave the bitch my gun."

Yemaya stared at Jimmy, her eyes ablaze with barely controlled rage and as black as coal. This was the man who shot Simtire. That alone would have been enough reason for her to kill him were it her place to do so. It was the images in his mind of his intended rape of Dakota that fanned her anger to dangerous levels.

"You will be quiet," she hissed, her voice seething. "Or I will order Simtire's pack to rip out your throat slowly and painfully and take great pleasure in making sure they take their time doing it. Do you understand me?" Yemaya demanded angrily.

Jimmy cringed and nodded. The woman's voice was like molten steel in his brain, burning hot and furious. He had no choice but to be quiet if he wanted the pain to stop and keep the wolves at bay.

"Good. You say another word, you move a muscle, you even think something I do not like and you *will* die, and the pain you just felt is nothing compared to what you will feel. This I promise. Regina and her pack would like nothing better than to tear you to pieces right now. You think about that for a while."

Jimmy nodded, feeling more afraid than he had ever felt in his entire life. It was a relief when she turned her attention back to Eddy.

"Why are you following me? Who wants me so badly they are willing to kill?"

Eddy knew he didn't want to answer her. He knew Chisholm would kill him once he found out he had been betrayed. There would be no place he could hide.

"It is okay, Eddy. Answer me. Who hired you?" she asked again, her voice calm, almost soothing.

Eddy sighed. It would be such a relief to just answer her question. He didn't owe Chisholm anything. Chisholm was an asshole. What did he care if she knew? She deserved an answer. It was Chisholm's fault Brenda Simpson had died and that Dakota had fallen over the cliff. Hell, if it hadn't been for him, Eddy might still have a life as a photographer. He now wished he had never met Robert Chisholm. He would tell her everything and Chisholm could rot in hell for all he cared.

"Robert Chisholm. He hired me."

"The publishing magnate? Why?"

"He never said. Just said to get as much information on you as I could. I could never please him. No matter how much I gave him, he wanted more. Not that there was much out there," Eddy added. "Next thing I knew, he wanted us to kidnap you and bring you back to his place. That's all I know."

"Call him," Yemaya ordered.

"Chisholm?" Eddy asked, shocked.

"Yes, call him. Tell him mission accomplished and you'll deliver his *package* to him in a week."

Eddy shook his head. This didn't make sense. Taking out his cell phone, he dialed Chisholm's personal number.

"Mr. Chisholm, this is Eddy. Yes, sir, she's...uh...with me right now. I have some information you'll be interested in...No, I'd rather not say on the phone...No, sir, I can't talk now...I...um...we'll be back next week...yes, sir...Just as soon as I arrive."

Snapping the lid shut, he looked at Yemaya.

"Good. You may go now. The wolves will lead you and the other two out of the forest. A van will pick you up by the road."

"You're letting us go? What am I supposed to tell Chisholm?" he asked, confused.

"I guess today is your lucky day," Yemaya answered. "You will know what to tell him when the time is right. Now leave before I change my mind."

"Come on, Jimmy, help me get Billy and Chuck moving."

"No, Jimmy stays." Yemaya motioned two wolves to guard him. "You and the others go."

"But what about Jimmy?" Eddy asked.

The look Yemaya gave Jimmy sent chills down Eddy's spine. Perhaps he was better off not knowing.

"Jimmy shot a wolf for defending what is mine, someone he intended on raping at the first opportunity. Were it up to me, I would kill him myself, but the wolves claim first blood right. His death will be painful, but justice will be served."

Eddy helped Chuck and Billy to their feet, then walked away, surrounded by three gray wolves. It was hard leaving Jimmy behind. Glancing back, he saw Yemaya walk toward

Jimmy. Already the three men were forgotten. Several more wolves appeared in the clearing. The image of the man being ripped apart nauseated him. A whisper in his mind scared him even more.

"Do not worry. Tomorrow, you will remember nothing."

Jimmy watched the wolves as they circled him and the woman. He had heard part of her conversation with Eddy but not all of it. Now she was standing in front of him, surrounded by several wolves. Eddy, Billy, and Chuck were leaving.

"Well, Jimmy, is there anything you wish me to tell your family?"

Jimmy shook his head. "Why would I want you to tell my family anything? And where are the others going?" he demanded, fear making him bolder.

"Home," Yemaya said unemotionally. "But not you. The wolves have a debt to settle. I could almost feel sorry for you, Jimmy...almost."

Turning her back, she walked away. The man's fate had been decided when he shot Simtire and thought about raping Dakota. There was nothing she would do to intervene on his behalf. The smell of urine was strong once Jimmy realized what was happening.

"Please, I'll do anything," he begged. "I don't want to die. Not like this. Shoot me," he pleaded, falling to his knees. "Please shoot me."

Yemaya kept walking, refusing to look back. If the wolves didn't kill Jimmy, she would. Her dark side demanded vengeance. She could feel the rage seething at being denied the opportunity.

Yemaya had defeated the darkness again, and it wasn't happy. One day, it vowed.

The wolves moved in for the kill. The growls, the ripping of flesh, the snapping of bones, and the screams of the dying man brought an unnatural stillness to the rest of the forest.

The creatures of the night understood and respected retribution. Justice was swift. One life ended and was quickly forgotten.

Dakota was dozing when Yemaya returned. It was only a few hours before sunrise. Yemaya knew she would have to tell Dakota some of the details but not all. Maybe in time, when Dakota learned more about her and her connection with the wolves and the land, she would understand and accept the darkness within her. She hoped so.

Reymone helped Raidon balance his demons. Hers were more powerful than his, but Yemaya was also stronger. With help from the woman she loved, the burden would be bearable and the demons could be controlled.

Slipping into bed, Yemaya curled her arm around Dakota's waist, snuggled against her back and slept. This time, she didn't wake up when Grandma Dakota appeared and spoke.

"Ya done good, chile. Sleep. The future gots many a path. It's yoh decision which ones ya take. Tonight, ya started down one that'll bring ya great joy ifn ya plays the cards right. Trust in my grandchile. She knowed good when she seed it, and she has mah strengths."

Smiling, Yemaya felt at peace.

"Thank you, Granny."

"Yoh welcome, chile."

"Oh, and, Granny?" Yemaya whispered in her sleep.

"Yes, chile. What is it?"

"I love you."

Grandma Dakota smiled.

"I luvs ya, too, magic woman. Now sleep."

Chapter Thirteen

Eddy looked at his watch. He had a two o'clock appointment with Robert Chisholm but wasn't exactly sure what he was going to say. The whole trip had been a failure, and now Yemaya Lysanne knew everything he knew about his boss. Eddy felt sure Chisholm would have him killed. Had he not felt compelled to meet with the man, he would have disappeared like Billy and Chuck.

Eddy didn't even want to think about Jimmy. All he remembered was leaving the man with Yemaya. How he and the others found their way out of the forest was a mystery. The driver of an old van had discovered them hiking down the road and picked them up. Kerc told them they were acting strangely. At first, he was afraid they were possessed by demons but decided they were okay and drove the three to Cahul. Tickets were waiting for them at the airport. Eddy assumed Chisholm had made the arrangements.

Robert Chisholm was impatient. He had waited almost a week for Jones to get back with Yemaya Lysanne and his report. Jones seemed to indicate he had some valuable information. If it turned out to be useless, Chisholm was sure he could extract what he needed from the woman.

"About fuckin' time, too," Chisholm swore. "This obsession of mine has cost me over a hundred grand."

A buzzer sounded on his desk.

"What?" he demanded after pushing the intercom button.

His secretary informed him Jones was waiting to see him. Chisholm told her to send him in. Opening the door, she motioned Eddy into the publisher's office. For the first time in years, Eddy felt calm. What he needed to tell Chisholm would put an end to the years of misery he had suffered at the CEO's hands. The relief was overwhelming.

"Well, Jones, you have something to tell me?" Chisholm demanded.

"Yes, I have a message from Ms. Lysanne and something to show you."

"Well, what is it?" he snapped, irritated at the shorter man's calm demeanor.

"First, Ms. Lysanne sends her regards. She said to tell you Ms. Devereaux has turned in her resignation. She'll be freelancing from now on."

"I don't give a fuck about Devereaux. Get on with it. What else did she say?"

"She said it would be in your best interests to cease your endeavors in pursuing her," Eddy stated matter-of-factly.

"Christ, Jones. You told her about me?" Chisholm yelled, his face turning red as vessels bulged around his temples.

"It seemed the natural thing to do," Eddy replied, unimpressed by the man's temper. "Then I'm supposed to tell you she'll be watching you now and recommended you focus on your own problems. It seems your company is about to be audited by the government. Ms. Lysanne wanted you to know she also has connections with powerful people and she can be very influential if need be."

"That's it? I spent thousands of dollars and you come back with this bullshit? And I'm supposed to be impressed or intimidated by her message?" Chisholm scoffed. "She hasn't a clue as to who she's dealing with. I have money and power. I can buy just about anyone I want."

"Yeah, I suppose you can, Mr. Chisholm. That's why she said to show you this if I thought you wouldn't listen."

Eddy pulled out a gun, showing it to his boss. Chisholm turned white. His heart pounded when he realized Jones was going to use it.

"Uh, Jones, don't do anything stupid," he stammered, taking a step back. "I have money. I can make you rich."

"I'm not after your money, Mr. Chisholm. Don't worry. I'm not here to kill you. Just to let you know I now know how Ms. Lysanne does her illusions and to pass on her message is all."

Wiping his brow with a handkerchief, Chisholm took a deep breath, feeling relieved.

"Good, so why the gun?" he asked curious.

"Ms. Lysanne said you might not believe her when she said she had a lot of influence, so she asked me to give you a small demonstration along with a final thought. She said you'd understand everything afterward."

"Get on with it then," Chisholm ordered excitedly. Finally, he was going to learn her secret.

"Yes, Mr. Chisholm." Turning to look out Chisholm's window, Eddy stared at the blue sky. He felt good knowing he had almost completed his mission. "Ms. Lysanne said to tell you if you don't back off, you're next!"

Eddy never heard the sound of the gunfire. The bullet entered the front of his right temple, leaving a small hole but pushed out a large chuck of brain and skull through the back. Blood and gore splattered the room, covering the walls, floor, desk, and the man sitting behind it.

Chisholm watched in horror. The gun fell from Jones's lifeless hand, landing with a dull thud on the carpeted floor. His body sank slowly to his knees, eyes glazed, a serene smile. Tumbling forward, he fell face down and twitched. Blood oozed from the wound and soaked into the expensive carpet.

Chisholm felt something wet running down his face. Thinking it was sweat, he wiped it with his hand. When he started to dry his hand on his pants he saw the blood, pieces of skin, and gray matter clinging to his palm and fingers. Robert Chisholm's scream was heard two stories down and several thousand miles away. The message had been delivered loud and clear.

Grandma Dakota sat cross-legged staring into the blue-orange flames of the campfire. Ladyhawk was resting on her shoulder. Both watched the flickering images of the two mortals sleeping peacefully, the magic woman's arms wrapped gently around her granddaughter, their bodies snuggled tightly together.

"Rest well, younguns. Theys be darker times in stohr."

As if her very words conjured up the future, the shadowed face of something banished the vision of the two women, replacing it with its own.

"I seed ya, demon. Ya been after the magic woman and her kin fer a long time. Ya kilt her mama, skeering that mare of hern and ya same as kilt her papa, knowin' he couldn't lives without her. Well, this one be diffrent. And we be a watchin' close like now. The spirits ain't tolratin' yoh mischief-makin' much more, so leaves her and my kin be ifn ya wants to stays in this here place. No moh of them thar tricks like ya done at that thar seequarium thing. Ifn any more of yourn try harmin' what's mine, ya wisht ya was burnin' in the fahrs of hell cuz it be a lot more homey than that thar cold place ya be hidin' in now."

Grandma Dakota could feel the dark energy seething from hate and frustration. The spirits had thwarted its craving to possess the magic woman's kin for over a millennium. Now Yemaya was the most powerful of her people. It wanted her badly.

In a vision, the human spirit had seen the future of her great-great-grandchild. If the demon ever gained control over the magic woman, she knew the spirits would need her strength, Maopa, the river mosquito, the most powerful shaman the Sioux nation had ever known. Flicking her hand, she vanquished its image as if dismissing a child. Angry howls reverberated through the spirit world.

The shadows moved quietly into the light of the fire. The elder Dakota looked around, acknowledging each by name and inviting them to sit. The council convened to discuss the future of Yemaya and Dakota. Much depended on their union, not just for them but for the welfare of Yemaya's people.

Vyushir lay by the flickering flames, listening to the *taibhseah,* the vision seer called Maopa. She knew certain forces were conspiring to capture the souls of the magie femeie and her mate. Normally, the wolf spirit didn't get involved in the affairs of mortals, other than her own kind, but the alliance with the woman's ancestors had been forged through blood sacrifices by both her pack and the family of the mortal called Yemaya. Yemaya was the newest guardian of her kin. That made Vyushir's interest in her personal.

She was angered when the young wolf Simtire was shot. The pup had bonded with the magie femeie's life mate and was thus honor bound to protect her, no matter what the price. The price had almost cost the wolf pup her life. Vyushir demanded the right of blood debt.

Regina, the pack leader, relayed this to Yemaya, and even though the mortal could claim equal right of vengeance against the human, she acceded to the spirit's wishes. In return, Vyushir was obligated to protect Yemaya's life mate.

When Maopa sent the request to convene the council, Vyushir was duty-bound to attend. She was aware of the tremendous energy Maopa possessed. Although, the spirit woman was a mere pup compared to the wolf spirit's age, her wisdom was undeniable.

More important, though, she had been the protector of the forests and its creatures when she was human. She remained so after her death. Her energies were so strong, her spirit resisted the calling of the Great Beyond. No human had ever been able to exist in the spirit world for more than a few days. For that alone, Vyushir was content to listen to the spirit woman's reasoning for calling the Council of Seven.

Ladyhawk watched the spirits appear one by one at the eternal flames of the campfire. Comfortably nestled on Maopa's shoulder, her unblinking golden brown eyes stared into the darkness, able to detect the exact spot a spirit materialized.

Vyushir lay quietly by the fire, her silver fur glowing from the flame's reflections. Sarpe lay coiled contentedly nearby, soaking up the heat from the campfire. Ladyhawk cocked her head slightly, examining the orange and black snake spirit. Rarely did Sarpe attend council meetings. She had little interest in the matters of beast or mortal. Her kin normally kept to themselves. Sarpe's presence confirmed the hawk spirit's suspicions—Intunecat, the Dark One, had returned.

Across from Sarpe sat Ursa, talking softly with Arbora. The bear and the forest spirits lived in close harmony. They spent a lot of time together. Ladyhawk felt sure their relationship went beyond friendship. Most spirits were loners, unable to cross the boundaries separating species, but occasionally, two would form a bond similar to what mortals called love. No spirit talked as much as these two if they weren't joined to each other.

A shimmering to the right of Maopa caught Ladyhawk's attention. At last, Mari had come. Mari was undeniably the most powerful on the council and the most beautiful of spirits. Tall, silver-haired with flashing blue eyes, she moved like liquid mercury, gliding smoothly from the darkness into the light. Mari ruled all life within the oceans, seas, and lakes. She was the birth mother of the land, although she had relinquished her claim to it eons ago.

Her iridescent blue gown shimmered as she gracefully settled next to Maopa. Bowing her head slightly, she acknowledged each spirit by name.

"Ursa, you are looking well, as are you, Arbora," Mari said, her voice soft, husky, and cordial. Words flowed like a warm summer breeze moving lazily through a mountain meadow. "I see the two of you continue to enjoy each other's *company* very much," she added, her approval obvious in her brilliant smile and twinkling blue eyes.

"We are indeed, Mari," Ursa boomed, her voice deep and slightly gravely like the low rumble of the Earth when it shifts deep within its core.

Arbora laughed lightly, nodding vigorously, the dark green hair around her bare shoulders barely covering the small breasts and pale olive skin. She was perhaps the most optimistic of all the spirits and the most playful. Almost as old as Mari, Arbora was the eternal child. She loved everything. Even the Earth listened when she spoke. Many a time she had quieted the dark rumblings of the land when it spewed forth its anger at the living.

"Right as always," the forest spirit agreed, grinning happily. The words floated gently, like a small butterfly carried on the wind. "It's good to see you, Mari. It has been far too long since our last meeting."

Mari bowed her head slightly, acknowledging Arbora's sincere greeting and gentle rebuke. Turning, she watched Sarpe straighten two coils and raise her broad flat head. Black elliptical pupils surrounded by golden-flecked irises stared unblinking into the ice blue eyes of the water spirit. Only Mari could endure the cold, deadly gaze with immunity.

"Ah, Sarpe, you honor us with your presence, my old friend," Mari beamed, winking mischievously. Sarpe was always so serious. She was perhaps the most feared of spirits in the mortal world and with good reason.

"As do you, Mari," Sarpe replied, returning the greeting, her speech slow, deliberate, and barely louder than a whisper. Sarpe was next in age to Mari. She took control of the lands when Mari decided to give them up. In time, Sarpe grew weary of the responsibility. When she was blamed for the sins of mortals, she became indignant and abandoned her interest in everything but her own kind. The Earth was left to Arbora.

"Thank you. It is good to see you again. I have missed our long talks."

Focusing her attention on Ladyhawk and Maopa, Mari sat quietly for a few moments. She knew the hawk spirit well, but the human spirit was a stranger. Still the whisperings of her existence had carried on the winds, but she paid little attention to idle gossip.

"Ladyhawk, you look well also. I hear you have been busy of late."

"I have my moments," the hawk spirit chuckled, her voice high and throaty like the call of an eagle.

"And as always, you handle them beautifully." Mari grinned. "And you are Maopa," she said, turning to the final spirit.

"That be me, but I likes to be just Dakota to y'all," Dakota said, having waited for Mari to finish her greetings. "Maopa be my injun name ifn ya prefers that. I gather ya be the top spirit that runs these here meetins."

Mari smiled at the strange-speaking spirit. There were no language barriers in the spirit world, but each retained certain characteristics of its kin. The elder Dakota, however, had kept more than usual. Mari was intrigued by the small attractive blonde.

"Not really, Dakota. I haven't bothered much with the ways of your kind or the others in eons. Humans are a disappointment to me...and the others," she said, nodding in the direction of the five spirits around her. "They manage quite well without me."

"Maybe that be as it is, but I'm thinkin' ya might at least be a takin' some intrest in that thar youngun of yourn," Dakota admonished, pointing toward the fire.

Mari sat quietly, staring into the eternal flames. The others sat watching, amused at Dakota's audacity. Few had the courage to challenge the eldest spirit.

"By kin, you would be talking about Yemaya, I presume," she confirmed, arching a silver brow.

"That be the one," Dakota answered. "Ifn she had yoh silvery hair, she'd be the spittin' image of ya. No mistakin' that one's blood kin."

"Yemaya and her people are of the Earth now. They abandoned the waters long ago. She is no longer my responsibility," Mari responded, shaking her head slowly.

"Kin be kin no matter where thar reared. Ya ken't just toss them asides cuz they moves on," Dakota said. "Chillin grows up, and they makes their own way. That's how it be."

Mari frowned. There was truth in the spirit's words. Still she hadn't bothered with Yemaya or her kin in thousands of years, and they had managed quite well without her.

"As you say, that is how it is. So what is it you wish me or us to do now that you have our attention?" Mari asked, aware of the others' amusement.

Dakota looked at each of the spirits before answering.

"Weel, now...trouble's a brewin' for the magic woman and my grandchile, and even ifn ya thanks that thar be my problem, I senses dark forces be behinds this and thar's moh to this than meets the eye."

"I've heard whispers," Mari agreed. The others nodded also. "So again I ask, what is it you expect of us?"

"Ah, now that be a damn good question. To speaks the truth, at this moment, I expects y'all ta looks after yoh own, then ya be needin' to keep an eye on each other's in case they needs some help, too. Ifn ya each does that, then nothin' else need be done fer now."

Amused, Mari turned to the other spirits. Such a simple answer to so complicated a problem. This Dakota was going to bring new life to the council.

"So be it. What say you, sisters? Shall we do as Maopa—Dakota—suggests? I no longer rule over your lands or people. If you agree with our sister, you must be my eyes. You need but call and I will be there."

The five spirits nodded their approval. It would be good working together once again. It had been a long time since the council had convened.

"Very well. Is that everything, Dakota?" Mari asked.

"Fer now," Dakota answered, satisfied.

All the spirits except Mari, Dakota, and Ladyhawk vanished, each returning to her own domain.

"You and I will meet again soon, spirit woman," Mari promised, her voice dropping to a throaty, hypnotic level.

"That be for shore," Dakota agreed, her green eyes gleaming with amusement. "The magic woman shore do have yoh talents," she smirked.

Mari laughed when she realized she'd unconsciously tried to use her gift of influence on the other spirit.

"Sorry. I'm not used to being around spirits. It's been a long time," she explained.

"Nothin' fer ya to be a worryin' about. I seed what ya kin can do with that soft-spoke voice of hers...ya ken't be affectin' me the same."

"So I see," Mari laughed. "Well, Dakota, I must be gone. I look forward to our next meeting."

"Well, now, that thar sounds like something we can agree on. Ya takes care of yohself, Mari."

"You too, Dakota."

Mari shimmered from view, leaving Dakota alone with Ladyhawk.

"That be one good lookin' spirit, Ladyhawk," Dakota said.

"Yes, she has always been beautiful, Maopa. Her absence from our councils was a great loss. She was devastated when her people left the oceans for the mountains. It's good to have her back," Ladyhawk said sincerely.

Once back in her own realm, Mari assured herself that all was well before relaxing by the thundering waters of the Great Falls. The pool at its base remained unnaturally calm, considering the volume and the force of the water striking its surface. Staring into the smooth waters, she watched the image of her kin slowly uncurl her long limbs from around the warm body of the spirit woman's descendant. It was obvious that both women separated reluctantly—Yemaya's a conscious thought as she awoke at sunrise, Dakota's an unconscious one as she groaned, her hand reaching out to pull the taller woman back toward her.

Dakota felt Yemaya's withdrawal. The absence of her lover's warmth disturbed her even as she slept. Sensing Dakota's efforts to wake, Yemaya tucked the blankets around Dakota and leaned over to kiss her cheek.

"Sleep, my love," she soothed, her soft whisper assuring Dakota all was well.

Yemaya dressed in black jeans, a black sweater, and hiking boots. It had been a little over two weeks since Chisholm's men had tried to kidnap Dakota. Fortunately, the attempt failed, even though Dakota was injured in a fall from a cliff. She was still recovering from her injuries. Most were minor aches and pains from the impact. Simtire, her faithful wolf companion, was well enough to return to the pack but preferred the company of Dakota. Yemaya worried how the young wolf would take Dakota's departure.

Maria was making breakfast when her mistress strolled into the warm kitchen.

"Good morning, Maria. Any chance of getting a hot cup of coffee?"

Smiling, the housekeeper began wiping flour from her hands.

"No, do not stop what you are doing. I can get it, thanks," Yemaya offered, patting the older woman on the shoulder.

Pouring the steaming liquid in a cup, she picked up a stack of newspapers and walked into the study. Her mornings always started with a cup of coffee and scanning several daily papers from around the world. Rummaging through the stack, she picked up the *Miami Herald*. Leaning back in her recliner, she sipped the hot brew and began reading the front page headline.

"Man commits suicide at Wentworth Publications." *Late yesterday, Eddy Jones, an employee of Wentworth Publications entered the office of CEO Robert Chisholm, pulled a gun, and killed himself, police said.*

Chisholm's attorney, George Killian, said the man was apparently suffering from depression due to personal problems.

"Mr. Jones was obviously a very disturbed man. He entered the office on the pretext of offering Mr. Chisholm valuable information on a research project he was pursuing. Once inside, he pulled out a gun and told Mr. Chisholm he was tired of living, placed the gun to his head, and pulled the trigger. Mr. Chisholm is very distressed over this matter and has decided to take a temporary leave of absence from Wentworth Publications," Killian said.

When asked about rumors of a federal audit, Killian had no comment. Chisholm could not be reached for comment.

"I just bet he is distressed," Yemaya snickered. "Now all I need to do is figure out what I am going to tell Dakota."

As if by magic, the woman in her thoughts knocked lightly on the door.

"Am I interrupting anything?" Dakota asked, setting a breakfast tray on the coffee table.

"Not at all. What is for breakfast?" Yemaya asked, getting up to sit on the settee by Dakota.

"Eggs, fruits, homemade bread, juice, and *meat*!" she exclaimed. "Real meat, bacon to be exact."

Yemaya laughed at her enthusiasm.

"Well, you can have my share since you seem so excited."

"Woohoo!" Dakota snatched up a strip and poked it in her mouth.

"Mmm, heavenly," she sighed.

Smiling, Yemaya buttered a slice of bread and offered a bite to her lover. Dakota gently clamped her teeth around the bread and the other woman's thumb and finger. She licked the fingers with her tongue before releasing them and taking the bread to chew.

"Hmm....you seem to be feeling much better today," Yemaya observed, chuckling.

"Oh, I've been feeling better for a couple of weeks. Nothing like a lot of time in bed to heal the body," Dakota joked.

"Yeah, rest does that," Yemaya replied. "I've been meaning to ask you. What did your boss say when you turned in your resignation?"

"He wasn't happy. I still owe him for the advances on my assignment."

"How much? I can transfer the funds immediately," Yemaya offered.

"No, I can't let you do that. You're not paying my bills. I have money. I'll send him what I owe."

Yemaya chuckled at Dakota's exertion of independence. Reaching over, she ruffled the short blonde hair.

"Okay, just offering. I might have a proposition for you, though."

Dakota grinned.

"And just what would that be?" she questioned, wiggling her eyebrows suggestively.

"Well...that is worth considering but not what I had in mind at the moment. I was thinking more along the lines of your article. How about I give you an interview? Would that satisfy the debt?"

Dakota frowned.

"Probably but it would have to be a really good one. I don't want to disclose anything confidential about you or your people, though."

"How about a few pictures of the village? Some interviews with a few locals and I answer some of the less personal questions? I promise you will have an exclusive no one else has had and nothing important will be revealed."

"Great. I'll call him later today and tell him. I at least owe him that."

Maria knocked softly on the door before entering.

"Mistress, Kenyon is on the phone. He requests your attention immediately if possible."

Kenyon was the local magistrate of Taraclia. Although elected by the people, his family had held the position for over three hundred years. They were highly respected and trusted by most villagers. Yemaya took the phone, apologizing to Dakota.

"What can I do for you, Kenyon?"

Dakota watched as Yemaya's expression changed from casual to serious. It was obvious something was wrong.

"I see...When did she disappear?...Last night? Why was I not called immediately?...This is unacceptable. You know I am available at anytime under such circumstances...Keep the men looking until sunset...They are not to go into the woods after dark. I will send my own people to look for her...You are welcome...And, Kenyon, you are never to delay contacting me in the future if something like this happens again. Goodbye."

Yemaya handed the housekeeper the phone.

150

"Maria, have Andrei organize the men. A young woman has disappeared. We will need to search the woods."

"Yes, mistress," Maria replied, quietly shutting the door behind her.

"What happened?" Dakota asked.

"One of our young girls has disappeared. She visited a friend last night and never returned home. Hopefully, she just suffered some minor mishap and is holed up somewhere."

"Maybe she's with a boyfriend or ran away or something," Dakota suggested.

"No, she is a good child. Something has happened. My men will search the woods for her. I will see if the wolves know something."

Dakota was just beginning to accept Yemaya's special relationship with the wolves in her region. Their obvious affection for her and obedience was undeniable. On several occasions, she watched Yemaya wrestle with them, then without a word, everyone stopped, the wolves howled in unison, and ran into the woods. Curious, Dakota asked Yemaya what happened the third time they ran off.

"I sent them to check on Verdina and Balba. They have a litter of four pups, their first. The wolves love their young. Balba is Regina's sibling, so they are always minding each other's business."

"I thought wolf packs were very individualistic and territorial," Dakota said.

"In some parts of the world, they can be. Ours tend to have closer ties than most. Packs will split and divide, but they remain a family. Cross one and you cross them all."

"A warning?" Dakota asked.

"Not for you. You are family and Simtire's mistress now."

Surprised, Dakota looked down at the young wolf lying at her feet.

"Mistress? I thought she just considered me another member of her pack."

"Normally, you would be. For some reason, she chose to make you her mistress. Highly unusual and quite an honor actually."

"But why?" Dakota was stunned.

Yemaya merely shrugged.

"You would have to ask her. I have never known a wolf to bond to another human in such a way."

"Human? You make it sound like you are something other than that," Dakota joked.

Laughing, Yemaya reached out and wrapped her arms around the smaller woman, pulling her close.

"Merely a figure of speech, my love."

Dakota was beginning to wonder what other talents Yemaya hadn't disclosed.

Chapter Fourteen

The voices had been there forever—faint whispers painting tantalizing pictures of young women undressing for his pleasure, telling him all the wonderful things they wanted him to do to them. It was his destiny to fulfill their needs, their wants, and their greatest need was to please him.

Unfortunately, no one understood him. People eyed him suspiciously when he talked to himself. Crossing themselves, they quickly moved away. Others lowered their eyes to avoid the insanity in his. Recently, however, something had changed. He no longer heard several voices. Now he listened to only one.

He had never heard of Taraclia, but the voice told him his dreams would soon be fulfilled once he traveled there. The local library provided him the information he needed to make his plans. Afterward, it was only a matter of packing the few possessions he owned and driving four hundred kilometers to the village.

A small motel provided the only accommodations he required. Once settled, he waited for instructions. For three days, the voice remained quiet. Frustrated at the silence, he finally decided he needed to go for a walk. An hour before sunset, he noticed a young girl walking hurriedly down the cobbled street and up the dark alley.

"She is teasing you," the voice whispered softly. "See how she leads you into the darkness. She shows you the way to your dreams. No one will see you in the alley."

Grinning, he nodded and followed the girl.

"Tonight, you must only follow her," the voice advised. "See where she goes, what she does."

"When?" he asked, anxious to begin the fantasy.

"Soon, very soon. Tomorrow you must retrace her steps so you will know the best place to take her. See how her hips sway. She wants you," the voice murmured.

"Yes, tomorrow then."

He followed her through several alleys until she stopped at a small house on the outskirts of town. The man glanced nervously at the wooded darkness beyond.

"There is a clearing through the trees. A quiet spot only a short walk. It is a perfect place to fulfill your dreams, to fulfill her dreams. No one will find you there. Tomorrow you must search it out and memorize the location."

Drool ran down his chin as he thought about the girl. She was probably sixteen or seventeen. Reaching down, he began rubbing his crotch in anticipation. He would make sure he gave her everything she wanted. He could almost hear her begging him for more. The man returned to the motel room excited over the prospect.

"She is only the first," the voice promised. "There are many more waiting to please you if you obey me."

"Whatever you say." He would agree to anything as long as his fantasies were fulfilled.

The wolves were restless. They felt the presence of something unearthly moving through the forests. Had it been human, they would have either ignored it or investigated, but this was something powerful, something that had not visited their land in many generations. Now it was back, and the older wolves weren't willing to challenge it on their own. They needed their mistress.

Shina was too young to understand or believe in the danger. Night was her favorite time. She prowled the woods or ran the meadows, long legs pumping, lungs struggling to oxygenate the large muscles. That night, she heard the call of a young male wolf from another pack. His lonely cries begged her to join him in a romp amongst the trees. Deep within her, the need to respond was irresistible. The male was black, the tips of his coat lightly frosted in silver. Big boned and muscular, she found him acceptable. After circling each other for several minutes, she lunged at his throat, lips curled, fangs exposed. Playfully, he shouldered her aside.

Again, Shina attacked and again he simply turned his shoulder toward her, parrying her strike. Soon she grew tired and lay down. Panting, he strolled up to her and lay down too. They began licking each other's face contented. The male wolf was the first to sense its presence.

Hackles raised, he turned and stared at the trees to their left. A low growl rumbled deep in his throat. Shina couldn't tell what made her playmate uneasy but decided it was best to imitate his behavior. Standing, her eyes searched the darkness for signs of anything not of the forest. A shadow moved slowly between the trees toward the meadow. The scent was foreign to the wolves, reeking of perspiration and something else. In its arms was the smell of a human.

Shina whined and backed away. When the young male refused, she grabbed it by the fur and pulled. Now wasn't the time for bravery or stupidity. The mistress needed to know about this. The male snapped at her, standing his ground. His ties to the mistress were not as great as hers. He'd only heard of her from other pack members.

Shina gave a final growl before loping off in the opposite direction. She had traveled only a short distance when she heard the snarls and howls of anger and pain and finally nothing. Anguish made her want to raise her nose to the sky and howl. Fear kept her silent. Her journey back to the pack would take several hours. For the first time in her life, she was afraid of the dark.

Dakota picked up the newspaper Yemaya had put down. She immediately noticed the headlines about the suicide. Scanning it, she turned to Yemaya but said nothing.

"What?" Yemaya asked, feeling uncomfortable.

"You read this?" Dakota asked, tapping the paper with her finger.

"I noticed it earlier," Yemaya said hesitantly.

"Anything you want to tell me?"

"What is to tell? I would not believe everything I read. You know how reporters are," she teased.

"Yeah, and I know something about you now. Did you have anything to do with this?"

"If you mean did I somehow influence Mr. Jones's actions, the answer is yes and no. At one time, Jones was a good man. Unfortunately, Chisholm made him into someone he hated. I gave him a choice to be who he was or who he wanted to be. He made his own decision after realizing what he had become. I guess he chose what he wanted to be," Yemaya said unrepentant.

Dakota wasn't sure what to think. Obviously, Yemaya had done something to Jones. She couldn't bring herself to believe the woman she loved would do anything wrong, though. Still she had no doubt Yemaya would go to extraordinary lengths to protect her own. Shaking her head, she put the paper down. Love was about trust, she thought. There was no reason not to trust her.

"What about Chisholm? What happened to him?"

"Nothing. The paper says he took a leave of absence from his position. I imagine when he returns he is going to have to answer a few questions from federal auditors. It seems there are some discrepancies in his tax records," Yemaya said, taking another sip of coffee.

"How inconvenient for him," Dakota said sarcastically.

"Very."

"Okay, then."

"Okay?" Yemaya asked nonplussed. "That is it? Okay?"

"Yeah. Okay. I believe you," Dakota smirked. "Any reason I shouldn't?"

"Well, no. No reason," she answered, unsure about Dakota's unquestioning acceptance.

"Good. So what's on the agenda today?" Dakota asked, changing the subject, amused at catching Yemaya off-guard.

"The first thing is to get the men out to look for the lost tehara, young girl. The wolves will help me."

"Us," Dakota corrected.

"You are not coming. There is going to be a lot of hiking, and you are still recovering from your fall."

"I'm fine and I'm coming. If you leave without me, I'll just take Simtire and go looking on my own."

"I can order her to stay here," Yemaya countered.

"I don't think she'll mind you very much once she sees me taking off on my own. Short of tying me up—and don't go getting any ideas—I'm helping."

Yemaya sighed. Obviously, Dakota could be extremely stubborn. The idea of tying her up was enticing but not the way Dakota meant. Smiling, she began to imagine all the things she could do with the woman in a bondage situation.

"Hey," Dakota said, slapping the woman's arm. "I know what you're thinking. Save it for later."

It was the second time Yemaya actually blushed.

"All right. Get changed and bring a warm jacket. We will probably be out for several hours. Regina is waiting for us."

"But you haven't...oh, never mind. I don't even want to know how you called them. Back in a few."

Yemaya watched Dakota walk from the room. Immediately, Maria entered and shut the door.

"Mistress, the men have left to look for the girl. The wolves are outside. Regina seems extremely agitated. I think she knows something."

"I am afraid so, Maria. Ms. Devereaux will be accompanying me today, so please pack a light meal for later."

"Beg your pardon, mistress, but is it wise to take the young lady with you?"

"No, not wise, but it is that or leave her here, and she has already told me she would go looking on her own."

"That young woman has a mind of her own."

"Indeed. I fear she is going to give me a lot of heartburn, Maria," Yemaya chuckled.

"I'm afraid so, but I think the benefits will far outweigh your frustrations," Maria said. She was happy for Yemaya. Her mistress had spent her entire life as a loner. If Dakota brought her peace and happiness, Maria would welcome her warmly.

"They do, Maria," Yemaya agreed, thoughtfully. "They do."

Regina paced back and forth along the fringe of woods, just beyond the drawbridge. When Yemaya and Dakota appeared, she immediately ran to Yemaya, stood on her hind legs, and placed her front paws on the shoulder of the woman. Golden brown eyes stared into icy blue. Moments passed. Dakota remained quiet, aware something important was going on.

After a few minutes, Regina dropped back to the ground and backed off. Yemaya knelt, beckoning a young female wolf forward. Shina crouched low and crept toward the mistress.

"It is okay, Shina. Come here." Again, Yemaya lowered her voice until it became soft and soothing. For a moment, Dakota felt herself drawn to Yemaya. It was an eerie feeling.

Shina stood and slowly walked forward. Yemaya stroked her head and rested her cheek against the wolf's head for a few seconds. Then she stood, wiping the dirt from her knee. Taking a deep breath, she looked at Dakota.

"Are you sure you want to come? It will be a long trek."

"But that's not what's bothering you, is it?"

"No. Something terrible has happened. We must hurry."

They moved quickly south, the wolves surrounding them as they led the way. Regina walked on Yemaya's right, Simtire on Dakota's left. Voinic was about fifty meters in front. Shina and the rest spread out and continually checked for anything unusual. The mistress and her life mate were now under their protection.

Unconsciously, Mari nodded in approval. The young mortal was a good match for her kin. Yemaya was a curious blend of strength and fragility, although no one would have guessed the latter. Her childhood had been far too short.

The death of her parents weighed heavily on her. She had been left to care for her younger brother, run the estate, and fulfill the obligations of her position.

When Raidon was old enough, he assumed much of the responsibility of managing the estate and their people. He had watched his sister grow lonely in fulfilling her duties, not that she ever complained. To outsiders, they seemed more like business partners than brother and sister. Outwardly cool and efficient, few caught the underlying teasing in their conversations, and even fewer understood the strong bond and love between them.

When Raidon was eighteen, he informed Yemaya he wanted to see the world before settling down. Longing to do the same, she understood his need. Three years later, he returned with a young man in tow named Reymone. They had been partners ever since. Reymone was one of those happy people in life, always laughing and joking. His favorite pastime was teasing Raidon until he either frustrated him completely or laughed good-naturedly at his antics.

Always the prankster, no one would have guessed he was a brilliant accountant and stock market analyst. The Lysanne fortunes had never been in danger of depletion, but Reymone ensured they would be around long after they and their great-grandchildren were gone. It was Reymone who suggested that Raidon take over Yemaya's duties, allowing her to fulfill her own dreams. Reluctant at first, she finally gave in and agreed to take time off. After instructing Raidon and Reymone about the affairs of the estate and the town, she began her own journey.

Years later, she made her debut in the United States and Canada as an illusionist. The occupation suited her nature and her needs. She could go anywhere she wanted, have access to anyone of importance, and look for any Carpi who might be abusing his or her power. Her travels, however, did not decrease the loneliness.

Mari felt a deep sorrow when she realized Yemaya had spent her life so alone. She too understood the desire to have someone. She had lived an eternity without companionship, excluding the spirits that constantly invaded her realm with their petty gossip or complaints.

"Invade be it?" a voice asked, interrupting her thoughts. Looking away from the pool, Mari watched the human spirit materialize next to her and plop down on the banks of the lake.

"Ya calls this invadin'?" Dakota teased.

"And hello to you, Maopa," Mari said, intentionally using the Sioux name.

"Ah, so ya wants to be that way, eh?" Dakota chuckled. "And what name does ya wants me to call ya? Mari? Gaia? Yemaya?"

"Touché, Dakota. But never Gaia. She is another. Now what can I do for you?"

"Well, I thoughts I'd just mind yer bizness. See ifn ya has decided to do right by Yemaya and her kin," Dakota asnwered, a small smirk appearing.

"Do right by her, eh? That sounds almost incestuous," the spirit teased. "Am I to get no peace and privacy in my own realm?"

"Ifn ya wanted thet, I wouldn't be here now, would I?"

Laughing, Mari could only shake her head. It felt good. She hadn't laughed out loud for eons.

"I guess you wouldn't. So what do you recommend I do?"

"Looks like ya already started. I seed ya watchin' them two. They be somethin' else, ain't they? The magic woman takes after ya. A right purty woman with a brain in that thar head."

"Yes, she is very beautiful and intelligent. Your great-great-granddaughter is equally so. They make a good pair."

"Fer shore. There be magic between them. Theys gonna be strong together. But I seed they be a needin' that strength—and ours," Dakota warned.

"I'm afraid you're right. I've been away from my people far too long. I forgot what it's like to feel," Mari admitted sadly.

Dakota patted the water spirit's leg.

"Ya hasn't forgotten. It just be a sleepin' in ya, but I thinks it be woke up now. I be a wonderin', though. How come you and they went separate ways?"

"It's so long ago, I'm not sure even I remember how it happened. At first, when they left the oceans, they lived by the shores. The oceans gave them food and tools. The land provided them shelter and clothing. It was a balanced union and life was good. Eventually, though, they moved inland, and soon the seas were forgotten, and with them, me. They claimed the land as their birthplace, and in time, I lost interest in them."

Shrugging her shoulders, Mari stared longingly into the clear water of the lake, watching the images of the two mortals guarded by the wolves.

"Perhaps I gave up too easily."

"Well, ya knowed when chillins leave the nest, ya has ta let them go. I knowed how painful that be. But they still be yer kin. Doesn't mean they don't luv ya, but they has ta live their own life. Ya seed that with all yer other chillin. Maybe ya jest cared too much and couldn't stand ta seed them gawn."

"Perhaps. It's too late now for regrets, though. As you once told me, it bes as it is," Mari said, trying to lighten the situation. "So now that you've invaded my realm, I might as well show you around."

"Might as well. Ya gots anything ta eat around here? I still likes to pretend to eat, ya knowed. Keeps me well rooted."

Laughing, Mari stood and held out her hand to assist the human spirit to her feet. Dakota took it willingly and immediately felt the spirit's warmth. Green eyes twinkled as she was pulled up.

"Thank ya, ma'am," she said, bowing at the waist.

Mari tipped her head slightly.

"You're most welcome. Now let's get you something to eat. Don't want you becoming unrooted, now do we?" she joked.

The two spirits moved away from the pool, the images in the water temporarily forgotten.

Chapter Fifteen

The voice was right. The meadow was perfect. It was a good hour and a half walk from town. Carrying his prize would be exhausting, but the adrenaline rush from his anticipation would provide all the energy he needed to get her there. Now it was only a matter of waiting for her to appear so he could follow her. The previous night's route would work well, but it wasn't necessary as long as she kept to the general area.

Returning to his room, he lay down to rest. The voices were quiet now, having been driven off by the one voice. Closing his eyes, he fantasized about his time with the girl. It would be fairly easy to grab her without attracting attention. The people normally didn't venture out after dark. She seemed to be the exception. Perhaps being so young or living in this town made her less wary. Whatever the reason, he was grateful to the voice for giving her to him.

Of course he would have to make sure she kept silent until they reached the meadow. If she didn't cooperate, a light blow to the head would suffice. It would be easier on him if she just cooperated, but he knew she would probably resist.

After all, girls loved to play the game. They were raised to say no, but everyone knew they meant yes. His father taught him that. He smiled, remembering how his mother whimpered and begged, telling his dad he could do anything he wanted as long as he didn't hurt her or her son anymore. That was real power.

"I see you approve of my gift," the voice whispered in his mind.

"Oh, yes. She's a pretty thing," he answered. "I hope I don't have to wait long," he added, reaching down to rub his groin, drool seeping from between closed lips.

"Not long. She'll be out tonight just before sunset."

"Good."

"You must wait till she leaves her friend's house. Only then will you have the entire night to enjoy your new plaything," the voice warned.

"Why can't I just take her when I see her?" he questioned, excitement mounting.

"Don't question me. Have I not guided you well so far? If she doesn't appear at her friend's house, they will call the parents. Then an immediate search will begin. If you wait, the parents will assume she is delayed or staying over. It will give you many hours to get her away and many more of pleasure."

"Yes, of course. Good thinking. I'll wait."

"You are wise to listen to me. Now that I've helped you, you must help me."

"Anything. What do you want?"

The man listened as the voice whispered its wishes in his mind. Nodding, he smiled, then laughed loudly. The night couldn't arrive soon enough.

The young girl bid goodbye to her friend and waved. It had been fun talking about their futures once they graduated from school. Both agreed they would attend the same university and maybe in time travel together. The Internet had shown them the wonders of the world, and they were anxious to taste them.

Humming quietly, she walked down a small alleyway not paying much attention to anything. Her neighborhood never had any serious problems, just the petty larcenies, disputes, or misunderstandings common in such places. Everyone understood the master or mistress would resolve issues and punish the wrongdoers. As she turned a corner, an arm snaked out, wrapping around her neck. A broad hand clamped over her mouth as another arm circled her waist.

"Be quiet!" a man's voice ordered quietly. "I won't hurt you if you stay quiet."

Nodding, she allowed herself to be dragged backward down the alley, her eyes searching for someone to help her. No one was around to hear or see her. Once they were at the edge of the forest, the man swung her around to get a better look at her face.

Putting his finger to his lips, he motioned for her to remain quiet while he removed his other hand from her mouth. Immediately, she screamed. The man slammed his fist against her temple, then caught her body as she slumped forward.

"I told you to be quiet," he grumbled. "Now look what you made me do."

Picking up the girl's limp body, he walked into the woods toward the meadow.

Two hours later, as he approached the open spot, he was halted by the voice.

"Put the girl down! There are others out there," it warned.

"Others? You said no one would be here," the man hissed, lowering her to the ground.

"No one is. These are not human. Now be quiet and listen. I will help you get rid of them."

"Them?"

"Wolves. They are no match for you as long as you have me. Did you bring the knives like I ordered?"

"Yes," he answered, reaching behind his back to pull out two long sharp filleting knives.

"Now wait. One of the wolves is leaving. All the better. The young male foolishly thinks he is a match for a human," the voice laughed. The sound sent a chill down the man's spine, making the hair on his neck stand up.

"Such arrogance. The young are so easy to deal with. They haven't learned fear. This one will. Now go."

"And do what?" the man questioned, sweat pouring down his cheeks.

"Do what I say. He can't harm you. If you want your prize, you will do as you're told and not question me," the voice sneered.

Shrugging, the man stepped into the opening. The black wolf glared at the intruder and moved slowly forward, hackles raised, a low growl rumbling from his throat. Humans were weak and normally avoided wolves whenever possible. He felt sure this one would run.

Sniffing the air, he was revolted by the scent of the man. Sweat and fear oozed from his pores, giving him a foul odor. If he didn't run, he would be easy prey. It was only when he was about three lengths away that he caught the scent of something else—something dark and sinister. Looking around, he tried to locate its source but saw nothing.

Shaking his head, the wolf once again focused on the human, lips curled upward, white teeth gleaming in the moonlight. Crouching, he tensed his muscles and sprang forward. It wasn't until he was almost on the man that he saw the flash of silver in both hands.

Pain caught him by surprise as it shot through his right shoulder and left side. Twisting, he fell to the ground rolling, his feet scrambling beneath him in an effort to jump up. The scent of hot blood filled his nostrils—his blood.

Darkness closed in, making it difficult to see. His heart beat harder as he attempted to stand. The rank smell of the man and the foul smell of evil overwhelmed him as he felt something hard push into his belly. Howling, he snapped at the source of the pain. The feeling of something sharp pounding over and over again was the last thing he remembered before he died.

The man stabbed the still body over and over again, jubilant in his victory over the wild animal. Warm blood covered his hand and clothes. Laughing maniacally, lips frothing, he raised his right hand toward the heavens as a symbol of his victory. Blood dripped from the blade onto the wolf's body. Suddenly, he felt a chilly breeze surround him and pass through his body. Shivering, he dropped the blade and stood, unsure of what had just happened.

"Very good," the voice approved. "Now get the girl and fulfill your fantasies. Remember my instructions after you are done with her."

"I remember," the man muttered, irritated at the voice for interrupting his enjoyment. Picking up the girl, he carried her to where the wolf's body lay.

"At least you'll see what I did." Placing her so her head rested on the wolf's body, he watched for signs of consciousness. When her eyelids fluttered, he grinned and unzipped his pants. Pulling them below his knees, he felt a sense of power when the girl opened her eyes and stared at his engorged penis, her eyes wide with terror.

Vyushir relaxed at her favorite spot, a high cliff overlooking the Carpiathian Mountain Range. Although an inhabitant of the spirit realm, she preferred to dwell in the mortal world. The moon, the wind, and smells made her feel alive. Listening to her children singing through the night and watching them running free through the forests gave her peace.

Eyes closed, she was enjoying the quiet when a howl pierced the silence. Immediately, Vyushir jumped to her feet, looking for its source. Another cry and a whimper only she could hear told her the direction. Leaping from the cliff, she plummeted to the ground several hundred feet below, running toward the wounded wolf.

By the time she arrived, the young male was dead, his life force having passed into the Great Beyond. Over him knelt a man, his hand still holding the knife raised toward the sky in victory. Angered, Vyushir lunged at him. When her body passed harmlessly through his, she howled, her cries carrying her frustrations through both worlds.

Mari and Dakota were nibbling on an array of sea plants when the echoes of Vyushir's anguish interrupted their meal.

"The wolf spirit has lost one of her own," Mari said sadly.

"To lose one of yoh own be a great sorrow," Dakota said. "Ya'd think we'd be used to it now, but I still feels a sadness when it happens."

"It's been so long since I was in touch with my people, I've almost forgotten what it's like," the water spirit reminisced. "The grieving and the pain."

"We never forgets. Maybe we can hide it or puts it away somewheres, but it's always thar in us waitin' to get out."

"I know," Mari sighed. "Perhaps we should see if we can help Vyushir. She has always been especially close to her own."

The two spirits left in search of the wolf spirit.

Yemaya, Dakota, and the wolves had been traveling for about three hours. Dakota could tell Yemaya was deeply troubled but didn't want to interrupt the other woman's thoughts. Besides, she realized she wasn't completely recovered from her accident and was beginning to tire.

Yemaya was disturbed by Shina's revelations. Although the female was young, she was not easily frightened. Something had scared her badly the previous night. The fact the male hadn't returned to his pack meant he was either seriously wounded or dead. Most likely the latter. More revealing was the unwillingness of the wolves to search for him. Wolves were creatures of the night. It would take something extremely evil to keep them from aiding a fellow wolf.

Yemaya could feel Dakota's exhaustion.

"I need a break," she said, sitting down, her back against a tree. Patting the ground between her legs, she motioned Dakota to sit. "We are almost there."

Dakota sat and leaned against Yemaya's chest. Two long arms wrapped around her, pulling her against the warm, solid body. Closing her eyes, she was asleep in minutes, her head slightly turned so her cheek rested against the other woman's neck. Yemaya nestled her cheek against Dakota's and dozed, knowing the wolves would warn her if anyone approached.

The sound of running water woke Yemaya. Before her stood a magnificent waterfall, tall and wide. A rainbow rose upward from the silver pool at its base and disappeared into the mist swirling around the top. A breeze drifted across the pool and over the lake in her direction, causing the water to ripple.

"Beautiful, isn't it?" a soft voice to her right murmured.

Slowly, Yemaya turned her head. Before her stood a tall woman with long silver hair and deep blue eyes fringed with thick silver lashes. Her shimmering blue gown clung seductively to her slender body.

"Yes, it is," Yemaya replied. "Who are you?"

"I see you're very direct. That's good," the woman replied. "I am Mari."

"Should I know you?"

"No, at least not in the way you mean, Yemaya, but you do know me. Look close. Who do I remind you of?" Mari whispered.

Yemaya stared at the woman. Something about her was familiar. Mari smiled, her white teeth perfect. Chuckling, she held out her hand, offering it to Yemaya.

"Come. Let me show you."

Taking her hand, she helped Yemaya to her feet and led her to the lake.

"Look into the water."

Yemaya leaned over, examining her own image. Next to it was that of the other woman. The faces were similar. Only the color of the hair and eyes were different.

"You are me," Yemaya exclaimed, shocked at the likeness.

"No, you are me," Mari corrected. "At least a part of you is. Eons ago, your people paid homage to the ocean. It was their mother and their father, providing the sustenance they needed. Then they left and forgot the ocean—and me. In time, I forgot about them," she said sadly.

"You are Gaia, the earth mother," Yemaya whispered in awe.

"I am Mari, guardian of the oceans and all that is water. Some mistakenly refer to me as Gaia. I created the land so my creations could grow and become more than what they were. Many left the water. A few returned. Your people never did. When they moved inland, they abandoned the ocean, so I left them and the Earth in the care of other spirits. They made better caretakers than I."

"I am honored, Mari, and I am curious as to why you appear now, after all this time."

"It would seem the others feel I have neglected my duties, one annoying spirit in particular," she smirked.

"Now, why ya tellin' the chile something like that?" a voice asked from behind them. "Ain't it bad nuff she be a thinkin' I'm some kind of a nut without ya be a blamin' me fer bringin' her here?"

"Hello, Grandma Dakota," Yemaya said, smiling at the smaller spirit.

"Howdy, chile. I seed ya finally decided to nestle down with that grandchile of mine," Dakota teased.

"How could I not?" Yemaya grinned. "She is so much like you—irresistible."

"Uh-huh. That silver tongue of yourn won't be a workin' on me like it do on them thar mortals. Ya bes just like this here water spirit. She be a thinkin' she can use her tongue on me," Grandma Dakota joked, knowing how it sounded.

"Maopa, you can be so bad when you want to be," Mari gasped.

"That be so true. Maybe ifn yer lucky, I kin be with ya," Dakota smirked, her green eyes glowing mischievously. Seeing the ancient spirit blush amused her greatly.

Yemaya coughed. This was more than she wanted to know or imagine. Apparently, the two spirits were attracted to each other, even if they didn't realize it yet. Of course, considering they were ancestors to her and Dakota, she really wasn't surprised.

"Could you two just tell me what this is all about?" Yemaya demanded, trying to change the subject.

"Sorry, Yemaya. Maopa...Dakota thought you should be forewarned about the young child and wolf. What you'll find is more than the work of a madman."

"That be the truth, chile. Darkness be a tellin' this un what to do. Ifn ya don't stop him soon, they be more chillins harmed like her," Dakota added.

"Who is he? Where can I find him?" Yemaya asked.

"That's the problem we're having. He is cloaked in darkness. Protected by it. We can't find him," Mari explained.

"What is this darkness?"

"We believe it shields the Dark One, Intunecat, from our sight. He is as ancient as time," Mari replied. "Even older than me. No one knows when the light came or from where, but as it grew stronger, the darkness grew smaller. A battle ensued. It lost, the light won, and I was born. The darkness was never really defeated, though. Throughout time, it appears and reappears, trying to push back the light."

"I guess it's making another attempt now. This man, you say he's a tool. What can this Dark One hope to accomplish with just one man?"

"Not just one. He uses many people in many ways. You've already experienced his subtleness, how he can take something like simple curiosity and turn it into an obsession."

"You mean Chisholm? I thought he was just power hungry," Yemaya said.

"That be the truth, chile. An once Chisholm got whats he wanted, he'd used it fer no good. Intunecat sees people's weakness and feeds off it. Few kin withstands the pawer of his darkness. It takes their lives, then their blood, and finally their souls. But you and my grandchile together ya has what it takes to beat him."

"How can we beat something that strong and ancient if the spirits cannot even do it?" Yemaya challenged.

"You are Yemaya, blood of my blood. My strength is your strength. I am the mother of the oceans and the land. Your people have a saying. Carpi are born of the Earth. That is true now. You, however, are born of the land and the sea. In time, you will understand what it means to be Yemaya," Mari said proudly.

Yemaya thought about her ancestor's words.

"What about Raidon? He is my brother. Does that mean he also has these strengths you talk about? Can he help us?"

"Raidon is of the Earth. He is a man. His strength is great, but he isn't you. In time, he may be of assistance. Enough of this for now. You must return to Dakota. She's rested enough to move on, and you don't want to be out beyond midnight. Vyushir will make sure you are well guarded, but even the wolves are no match for Intunecat when it is on the prowl."

Yemaya felt Dakota moving in her arms and unfolded them from around her. Leaning close to her ear, she murmured softly.

"You ready to go?"

Yawning, Dakota nodded.

"Yeah. Was I asleep long?"

Looking at her watch, Yemaya shook her head.

"Maybe about twenty minutes. But we need to get a move on it. According to Regina, it is only another thirty minutes to the girl."

Yemaya didn't want to tell Dakota what probably lay in store for them. Still she felt her lover was entitled to know what she knew, not that she knew very much—only what the spirits had told her. It was enough to make her uneasy.

Standing, Yemaya helped Dakota to her feet. The wolves immediately took up protective positions around them and guided them toward the meadow. Thirty minutes later, they entered a small glen. The body of the young woman was lying as if asleep, her head resting on the stretched-out body of the wolf. One would almost think they were sleeping if it hadn't been for the bloody clothes, fur, and stains on the ground.

"Stay here," Yemaya ordered, turning to Dakota. "Please," she added, softening her tone.

Nodding, Dakota stood still, her hand stroking Simtire's head nervously. The female wolf whimpered. Yemaya, Regina, and Voinic walked over to the bodies. Yemaya knelt and touched the girl's cheek. Regina sniffed at the body of the male wolf.

Yemaya was sickened at what she saw. The throat was severed almost through the spinal column. Several slashes on the upper arm and superficial stab wounds to the exposed chest, along with the amount of blood on the body and ground told her the girl had been alive when they were inflicted. The slashing of the throat was probably the madman's last act. Yemaya didn't want to think about what else was done to her before she was finally killed.

As she was about to stand, she noticed something unusual about the chest wounds. Gently, she pulled back the girl's blouse and took a deep breath to control the rage growing inside of her. Carved across her breasts was the word drac. Yemaya picked up the girl's hand, closed her eyes and concentrated. Distorted images of a man cloaked in shadows carrying the girl's body flashed across her mind.

Over the next several minutes, she watched as the man undressed and stood naked in the meadow, his knife flashing in the moonlight. Then as the tehara slowly opened her eyes, confused, he sank to his knees between her outstretched legs.

Placing his hand over her mouth, he showed her the knife and shook his head. When she nodded, he removed his hand and slowly unbuttoned her blouse, enjoying the fear in her eyes. His arousal was obvious. Yemaya felt the girl's terror. She could smell the scent of the man, the sweat, the adrenaline. Perspiration poured down the girl's cheeks and she trembled. He laughed. It was the insane laughter of a madman. Drool ran from his mouth, down his chin, and dripped on the exposed breasts. Reaching down, he pulled up her dress and ran his hand up her thigh, while his other hand frantically rubbed his crotch.

"Yemaya!" Dakota screamed. "Yemaya, honey, turn loose," she said, grabbing Yemaya's hand.

Dakota had watched Yemaya and the wolves approach the bodies. Regina sniffed at the young wolf and backed away growling. Yemaya knelt to examine the girl. She was about to stand when Dakota noticed her hesitation. Yemaya's body stiffened momentarily, then she picked up the dead girl's hand. Dakota realized immediately something was very wrong and ran to Yemaya, calling her name. When Yemaya didn't respond, Dakota finally grabbed her hand, pulling as hard as she could.

Unable to dislodge Yemaya's grip, she panicked. Suddenly, Regina launched herself at Yemaya's chest, her massive weight and momentum knocking her mistress backward. Once the connection was broken, Yemaya lay still, taking deep breaths, her eyes closed tightly against the pain from the abrupt severing of the contact.

Dakota sat next to her. Picking her head up, she rested it on her lap. Regina and Simtire circled the two uneasily, while the other wolves patrolled the perimeter.

"Yemaya, sweetie, talk to me," Dakota said softly. "What happened?"

Yemaya could only shake her head, nausea crawling like worms through her stomach. This was an experience she couldn't fully share with her lover. The horror of feeling what the girl felt, seeing what the man had done left her feeling raw and vulnerable. For Dakota to know everything would accomplish nothing.

"Yemaya, please talk to me. Let me help."

"She is stronger than you give her credit for," a soft voice whispered in Yemaya's mind. "Trust in her."

When she opened her eyes, Dakota saw blue eyes darkened by pain and great sadness

"Tell me."

Sighing, Yemaya nodded but closed her eyes again. She couldn't bear to see the effect of the words on her lover. Slowly, she described the vision, her body trembling occasionally, while Dakota listened quietly.

How horrible it must be to relive something so awful, Dakota thought. Her concern for Yemaya exceeded her revulsion of the events being described. When Yemaya finished, she lay quietly for a few minutes soothed by the warm hand of Dakota as it stroked her hair. Finally, she made eye contact with Dakota and found concern instead of disgust.

"You never cease to amaze me," she murmured, her voice husky from the stress.

"Why is that?' Dakota asked, smiling slightly.

"I thought you would be shocked, horrified, and maybe...well...maybe..." Yemaya hesitated.

"Maybe squeamish and go all girlie on you because of what you saw or are you referring to your ability to see through the eyes of a dead girl?"

Yemaya nodded.

"Let's see. You're an illusionist who does tricks I've yet to figure out. You talk to wolves, and they apparently talk back. I suspect you have an ability to either plant ideas or control minds—to what level I don't know—and now this. Anything else you want to tell me?" she asked half joking.

"It would take a lifetime," Yemaya said, smiling in response.

"Then I suppose I'll be sticking around a while if I want to know everything."

"I suppose so," Yemaya agreed, relieved. Turning to Regina, she nodded toward the woods.

"Andrei is on his way here. He is bringing some men to take the girl home. We have to head back. The dead wolf's pack has arrived, and they will watch over the bodies until the men arrive. They should be here shortly."

"Do you have any idea who did this?" Dakota asked.

"Somewhat. Nothing definite, though. I had another dream while we were dozing. Seems the spirits are involved in our lives more than we think."

"Do tell," Dakota smirked.

On their trek home, Yemaya talked about the dream. When she described Mari and her questionable relationship with Grandma Dakota, Dakota burst out laughing.

"Why am I not surprised to hear you're related to a spirit?" Dakota teased. "That explains those many skills of yours."

"Maybe. That would also explain why my people are so different from other cultures. I think time has diluted their abilities, though. Probably a good thing, considering what they might have become had they kept the levels they must have had in the beginning," Yemaya said thoughtfully.

"Are any of them equal to you? Raidon?" Dakota asked.

"I do not think so, at least that is what Mari says. Raidon and I have never talked about it. I doubt he is ready to hear about these dreams we are having. He is a very practical person."

"You say that as if it's a bad thing."

"Not bad but quite annoying sometimes."

Standing, Yemaya took Dakota's hand and pulled her to her feet.

"Are you ready?"

Nodding, the two women followed Regina and her pack into the woods. Several young wolves paced restlessly near the bodies anxious to leave the meadow and the smell of death.

Chapter Sixteen

The man lay down to rest. The night had been better than he could ever imagine. If only the girl had been more cooperative, it would have been perfect. He expected her to beg, just as his mother had done with his father. Instead she refused. It was only when he made the small cuts on her arms that she broke her silence.

The screams were wonderful and excited him. Opening her blouse, he ran the bloody knife up and down her chest, painting her breasts with bright red streaks. He could feel himself getting hard again. Reaching between her legs, he ran his hand up her thigh. She trembled. When he finally exhausted himself, he straightened back up, still on his knees.

The voice had told him to kill the girl. His pleasure was so great he really didn't want to, but he had agreed, and he wanted to keep the voice happy. Reaching down, he grabbed the girl by the hair, pulling her head back. Raising the knife, he slashed her throat quickly and as hard as he could. The blade partially jammed in the neck bone.

"There," he muttered. "Now this won't hurt."

Quickly, he carved the word drac across her chest. Such a waste, he thought.

"I know I could've made you beg."

For a moment, he was angry at the voice for making him end the fun so soon.

"Well, it owes me now," he mumbled.

It took less than two hours to walk back to his motel room. The sun was just peeking over the mountains. Several people were already in the streets on their way to work or to run personal errands. No one paid attention to him as he slipped inside his room. He took a quick shower and tossed his soiled clothes into a bag. Later, he would discard them in some trash container a few blocks from the motel.

"You are pleased with my gift?" the voice asked.

"Yeah, she was nice," the man answered. "Shame I couldn't have kept her a while longer."

"There will be others," the voice promised. "Now you must rest. I'll let you know who the next one will be."

"How long do I wait?"

"Patience. The townspeople will be looking for the girl's killer. You must appear normal. Show concern when you hear the news, but stay away from the Lysanne family, especially the one called Yemaya."

"How will I recognize her?"

"Tall, dark-haired, blue eyes, self-assured. You will know her when you see her, and she will know you if you ignore my warnings."

"I'm tired of talking. Leave me alone so I can rest." the man whined.

The laughter was chilling. The voice deadly.

"Careful, my friend. I don't take orders from the likes of you," it hissed.

"Sorry," the man muttered.

Andrei, along with a few men from town, arrived shortly after Yemaya and Dakota left the meadow. After saying a prayer and crossing themselves, two men wrapped the girl in a blanket, gently lifted her body, and walked away. Once they had left, Andrei knelt by the dead wolf. He stroked the black head several times, tears streaming down his cheeks.

"Rezem atoare, ale meu prieten."

Sliding his hands under the body, he lifted the animal in his arms, cradling it as he would a child and walked in the opposite direction. He would bury the wolf in his pack's territory and say the ritual prayer, sending his soul to the Great Beyond.

Andrei's family had served Yemaya's family for hundreds of years. He understood the alliance between the Lysannes and the wolves. His father and his father's father had taught him their ways. Although he wasn't able to communicate with them like his mistress, he understood what they wanted and their needs. Perhaps his family's closeness to the Earth and the mistress had given him a special gift. Whatever the reason, he lived and would die for them. Such was his love of both wolf and mistress.

Yemaya and Dakota arrived home a few hours before sunset. Maria had a warm meal waiting for them in the study.

"Do your people read minds, too?" Dakota asked, seeing the hot porridge and fresh bread already laid out on trays.

"No, at least I hope not," Yemaya laughed. "But Maria has always been able to sense my arrival. I guess she has some abilities, though."

"Figures. This looks really good."

Serving the porridge in bowls and slicing some bread, she carried the tray to Yemaya. They quietly ate the meal, each lost in her own thoughts about what had happened, unaware of the passing hours. The silence was interrupted by a knock on the study door. Andrei walked in, bowing slightly to Dakota before turning to Yemaya.

"He is home now, mistress."

"Thank you, Andrei. Regina and the packs appreciate you returning him to his family," Yemaya said softly. "What do the men say?"

"They're in shock, mistress. Nothing quite like this has happened before. Some fear the drac has returned, while others say it is the workings of a madman."

"I fear they may both be right, Andrei. Get something to eat and rest. I know this has been hard on you. Tomorrow we will see if we can discover who or what is behind this abomination."

Andrei tipped his head and again turned to bow to Dakota before leaving.

"I don't know about you," Dakota said, "but I'm exhausted. I think I'll call it a night."

"Good idea. I can check with Maria to see if anything needs tending to, then be right up."

Yemaya walked into the warm kitchen. The smell of baking pastries filled the air.

"Evening, mistress," Maria greeted. "'Tis a sad day for our people and the wolves."

"Yes, it is, Maria. Hopefully, we will discover who did this before it happens again."

"You don't think it's a one time thing then?"

"No, this is just the beginning if we do not find this madman."

"Andrei says the townspeople are afraid the drac has returned." Maria crossed herself.

"I fear they may be right. Something about this does not feel natural to me," Yemaya said but didn't elaborate. "I am going to get some rest. Have a good night, Maria."

"You too, mistress."

Dakota was already in bed half-asleep, snuggled under the quilts. Yemaya slipped in next to her, wrapping her left arm around the smaller woman's waist and pulling her close. Her hand snaked under the tank top and pressed gently against Dakota's stomach before making slow circular motions.

Placing her lips next to Dakota's ear, she blew softly, her warm breath caressing the lobe and entering the canal. Dakota shivered as the hand roamed up to her breasts, the fingertips lightly touching the left, then circling the right before finally settling on the right nipple. Thumb and finger stroked the nipple and tugged on it.

"You too tired?" Yemaya asked, her voice husky with desire.

Dakota rolled on her back and captured Yemaya's gaze.

"With you? Never," she murmured. She reached up and pulled Yemaya's head down, her lips claiming Yemaya's, the tip of her tongue tickling Yemaya's lower lip.

Yemaya opened her mouth slightly and touched Dakota's tongue with her own, breathing in the scent of her lover. Her own breathing was ragged. She didn't have the patience to go slow and easy. She wanted to take Dakota with passion and fire; she needed to wipe out the earlier memories.

Yemaya kissed her way down Dakota's body, stopping at each breast to taste the skin before moving on. Her hands followed her lips, palms spreading to cup breasts, fingers kneading them gently before sliding down the ribs to Dakota's full hips. Slipping her hands beneath the buttocks, she pulled Dakota toward her as she moved to position herself between the woman's legs. Leaning back, her eyes roamed the partially covered body.

"Time for these to go," she whispered, pulling first the tank top off Dakota, then her shorts. Pale blue eyes darkened as she looked at the sleek body beneath her. Bending down, she ran her tongue through Dakota's pubic hair, swirling it in small, slow circles. She could feel Dakota's legs trembling in anticipation.

"Tell me what you want," she demanded.

"You...inside," Dakota gasped. She groaned when she felt fingers inserted into her vagina. They moved slowly, twisting slightly back and forth as they pushed in and out. The other hand pressed firmly on her pubic area. Dakota's hips picked up the rhythm of the fingers, coaxing them to move faster and harder. Yemaya leaned forward, resting her head on Dakota's belly, her hand thrusting vigorously.

Dakota moaned loudly. Yemaya had found a particular spot that was driving her crazy. Waves of indescribable pleasure coursed through her body every time a finger touched that area.

"Oh, fuck," she cried, her body arching as her heels pressed into the mattress. Grabbing Yemaya's wrist, she pushed it hard against the sensitive spot.

"Please..." she gasped, barely able to speak. "Hold it there...don't...move."

Yemaya obeyed immediately.

"Am I hurting you?" she asked.

"No...no..."

Yemaya continued applying pressure to the spot, aware Dakota's hips were pressing hard against her hand. When the trembling set in, she moved her other hand under Dakota's back and repositioned herself so she could support the smaller woman's body.

Spasms racked Dakota's body as waves of pure pleasure moved from her center outward. Her muscles tightened. The muscles of her vagina locked around Yemaya's fingers, squeezing them until they almost ached. A sudden release of fluid warmed her hand. Almost instantly, Dakota's body relaxed and she groaned.

"Jesus fucking Christ," she moaned, gasping for air.

Yemaya slipped her fingers out and dried them on the sheets before reaching up to stroke the blonde hair. Exhausted, she lay next to Dakota, leaning in to kiss her cheek.

"You are amazing," she whispered, her voice soft and silky.

"No, you...are amazing. I've never felt that before. I can't even describe what I was feeling, but it was...I don't even have the words to tell you what it was."

Yemaya smiled, satisfied. Her eyes closed. She felt Dakota move and opened one eye to see what was going on. Dakota was grinning wolfishly at her.

"You think you're getting off that easily?" she asked.

"Uh..."

Dakota grabbed a handful of long dark hair and pulled Yemaya's head back, exposing her throat. Slowly, deliberately, she ran her tongue across her lower lip. Then dipping her head, she nipped at the bared throat.

"My turn."

Yemaya watched the blonde head move around her chest, stomach, and navel and down to her groin. She could feel the moisture running between her legs. When two fingers stroked the outer lips of her vagina, her legs automatically spread wider, inviting Dakota to continue. The back and forth motion of the fingers sent chills up and down her body. She wanted Dakota inside her now.

Sensing what her lover wanted, Dakota smiled smugly, refusing to grant Yemaya's wish. She would continue to torture her for a long time with fingers and tongue before granting Yemaya the relief she craved.

Hours later, the two settled into a deep slumber, tired from the day's activities and their night of passion.

"At last we meet." The voice was low, melodic, and soothing. At first, Dakota thought Yemaya was talking to her and was confused by the strange comment. Opening her eyes, she became aware of the sounds of water thundering a few hundred feet away. She turned, seeking its source, and saw an enormous waterfall.

"Beautiful, isn't it?"

Dakota shifted her position to look at the woman talking to her. If it weren't for the silver hair and eyebrows, she could have been Yemaya.

"You're Mari, aren't you?" It was more a statement than a question.

Mari tipped her head slightly, acknowledging the observation.

"And you are Dakota," she replied. "Welcome to my world."

"Yemaya told me about you. She said you two looked alike. If it wasn't for the hair and eyebrows, I would've mistaken you for her."

"Well then, I guess it's a good thing we have that difference," Mari teased.

Catching the innuendo, Dakota blushed. Apparently, Mari knew of their relationship. Then again, there probably wasn't much she didn't know, considering she was the water and Earth mother.

"I don't intrude into bedrooms," Mari assured, reading the mortal's thoughts. "But I have watched and listened to you on occasion. I'm aware of the bond between you and my distant daughter."

"That bes for shore," her grandmother Dakota confirmed.

"Grandma," Dakota exclaimed, jumping to her feet to embrace the elder woman. "I wasn't sure I'd see you again."

"Now, now. I'll always be with ya, chile."

Mari watched the two embrace and smiled. They too were alike except that the elder Dakota looked older. Still, she was very attractive, and her speech was so unique.

"I'm sorry to interrupt your reunion, but the council is waiting," Mari said.

"Best we gets a move on it. The sun be a peekin' through them mountains already."

Sarpe, Arbor, and Ursa were gathered around the Eternal Flames. Ladyhawk immediately appeared on the elder Dakota's shoulder, and Vyushir shimmered in shortly afterward.

"Welcome again, my friends. Vyushir, we feel your loss."

Vyushir bowed her head slightly, acknowledging Mari's condolences.

"Friends, I bring you Dakota, daughter to Maopa," Mari continued, introducing each spirit.

"Why do you bring thissss mortal to the councccil?" Sarpe hissed, her voice low and hypnotic. "The magic woman holds the power. Thissss child is young and inexperienccced."

The others nodded their agreement. Other than her relationship to Maopa, she was merely human.

"A fair question, Sarpe," Mari answered. "Dakota doesn't have the powers my daughter has, but she is the key that unlocks Yemaya's full potential, and she is the control that keeps it in check.

"Yemaya has known for a long time that immense power dwells within her, and she wisely refuses to use it. Had she done so before meeting Dakota, she would have fallen prey to Intunecat. We all know by itself power is neither good nor evil. It is merely a tool that exists only to be used by the holder. In the case of mortals, there has never been one so good as to be immune to its influence. Yemaya is strong, but even she will succumb to its seduction with the Dark One's help."

"That be the truth. The magic woman knowed her strengths and failins. Twernt no reason to bring her here. It bes this un that needs ta knowed how important she be and ta sees what they bes up against."

"But does Yemaya know this mortal is the key if it is so?" Ursa growled in her deep gravely voice.

"She suspects, but she doesn't accept it completely. My daughter will do anything to protect Dakota. This may jeopardize both of them."

"Do you understand what we say?" Mari asked, turning to Dakota, who had remained quiet during the conversation.

"Not entirely, but I have a pretty good idea."

"All you need to know is you must remain strong. Yemaya will resist your involvement in this out of fear for you. Do you have the strength to stand up to her?"

Dakota laughed softly and nodded.

"I'll do everything humanly possible to protect her, even if it is against her own stubbornness. She is my life, my breath."

The spirits were satisfied. This mortal would die for her life mate if need be. They would do their best to make sure it didn't happen.

"We will do what we can to assist you," Arbora said. "The forest is our eyes and ears. But be forewarned. It wasn't the young girl's spirit your life mate merged with. The Dark One wanders the shadows, even those of the mind. He isn't easily seen, and he is not what he seems. Even I can't find a shadow behind a shadow, and my world is filled with them."

"True," Ursa growled. "If Intunecat plants his seed within Yemaya, she will be his to rule, and all will be lost. You mustn't allow this."

"Plants his seed?"

"She means if he can gain control of her mind, Dakota," Mari explained.

"Oh. It'll never happen."

"My people sssee well in the dark," Sarpe said. "We may not ssssee the shadow, but we can tassssste where darknesssss travels or hides if it is near.

"And mine have sharp eyes," Ladyhawk said. "We'll watch for signs of Intunecat wherever my people fly."

"If any of your people find signs of the Dark One, you need only whisper into the wind. The news will reach me, and we'll unite and make better plans. Until then, be well and safe, my friends," Mari said.

The others vanished, returning to their own worlds.

Dakota watched her grandmother stand and reach down to assist Mari to her feet. Mari looked amused at the gesture but willingly allowed the human spirit to pull her up.

"Thank you, Maopa." Her eyes twinkled with humor. "You are most kind to assist one as old as me," she joked.

Dakota would have sworn her grandmother actually blushed but refrained from teasing her. If spirits could love, these two were well on their way to such a journey. She was happy for both of them.

"Well, I guess I need to be getting back," she offered, feeling a little ignored as the two spirits stared into each other's eyes.

"That be true, chile," the elder Dakota agreed. "The magic woman feels yer absence and bes restless. We bes meetin' soon."

Hugging her grandchild, Maopa stepped back, allowing Mari to say her farewells.

"Be careful, Dakota. The Dark One wants Yemaya. She could be the one to tip the scales in his favor if he succeeds."

"If he succeeds, it will be over my dead body and spirit," Dakota declared vehemently.

"So be it," Mari said.

Dakota awoke to find Yemaya moving restlessly in her sleep. She stroked her lover's hair while making soothing sounds.

"Shh...shh...it's okay, baby. Sleep."

Immediately, Yemaya settled into a peaceful slumber.

FRAN HECKROTTE

Chapter Seventeen

Intunecat stormed through the darkness. The spirits were once again interfering with his right to reign over the land and peoples. By right, they belonged to him. He was the Firstborn. Darkness had ruled the worlds long before the arrival of light. They were the interlopers. What right did they have to push him back into the confines of shadows? He was tired of living in the darkness. Even he enjoyed the light for short periods. Had it not been for him, they wouldn't exist, he mused.

He remembered the age of total, endless darkness. No one could understand how black the night was—no stars, no suns, nothing. He never knew when he became fully conscious of his world. All he remembered was the loneliness. A loneliness so complete he ached for something, for someone, and so he toyed with the elements.

During one episode, he noticed a white flicker. Curious, he reached out to grab it and felt an immediate burning sensation in his palm. Instinctively, he tossed the fleck away, then watched it expand until its glow began eating away at his own world. He could do nothing to slow its growth, but in time, it subsided and eventually stopped. His world had shrunk to half its original size.

Then came Mari. For eternities, he lived alone in the darkness and suddenly he felt a presence from within the light and she was beautiful. Unfortunately, he dared not venture there. If the initial speck was any sign of its potential, he could be incinerated, and she avoided the dark.

Soon, others arrived to keep her company, which made his loneliness even greater. Through the eons, he grew angrier and more embittered. Still he preferred their distant company to his solitary existence from before. After all, what was a kingdom without subjects?

With the help of Mari's descendant, he could take his rightful place. She had the power to alter the thoughts and feelings of mortals, although she rarely took advantage of it. Why, he never understood. Such power was a gift to be used, not ignored. His own abilities only worked with people already tainted by darkness. The concept of evil escaped him. He had needs. Right or wrong was never an issue. They had companionship. He only had the darkness. He wanted what they took for granted.

Intunecat could control the dark side in humans. The few who didn't have one or only a small darkness were immune to his influences, but not to Yemaya's. This human was unique. She was the catalyst to his aspirations. Now not only were the spirits defying him, but another mortal was interfering with his plans to control Yemaya.

Intunecat had been so close to his goal when she touched the dead girl. She thought she had merged with the girl's spirit when in fact she was seeing and feeling his projections. A few more seconds and he would have gained entry into her subconscious, just as he had with the man. Then she would have been his. But the other mortal, with the help of the queen wolf, broke the connection before he could plant the seed of darkness. Cursing, he slammed his fist into the darkness. Loud thunder rumbled through the skies from the impact.

Intunecat watched the man carry the girl's body home. He could smell everyone's fear, something he could use against them. As humans evolved, they grew afraid of the dark. Why, he never understood, but it allowed him to pursue his own agenda.

Eventually, however, other things hid amongst the shadows, feeding off the fears of humans. Some were not satisfied with just the fear but chose to survive on the blood, energy, and souls. These creatures disgusted him.

Vampires were real as were many other sordid creatures of the darkness. Fortunately for humans, they were few and far between, preferring to keep to themselves. Most were solitary, distrustful of everyone and everything, even their own kind. Contrary to popular belief, vampires could move around in daylight for a few hours. Garlic had no effect, and crosses were about as useful as garlic. They were not the undead. It was true they propagated by exchanging blood with their victims but rarely did they convert a human. The danger to them was too great. An offspring could easily find its creator once it completed the transition.

Intunecat could destroy the species, but it served a purpose. It kept humans afraid and perpetuated their fears of the darkness. That gave him the control he needed for the creation of his reign.

Intunecat took no pleasure in killing. Death was for mortals. What lay beyond it even he did not understand, but he knew how most humans reasoned. Had he simply let the man satisfy his needs, the girl would have returned home to be comforted by her friends and family. The man would eventually be caught, labeled insane, and imprisoned. By instructing him to kill and mutilate her body, it brought Yemaya to the site. He knew she would use her powers to see the event as it unfolded.

Doing so provided him with the opportunity he needed to enter her mind. Her life mate's interference caught him unawares. She would have to go. It wouldn't be easy now that the spirits were involved. Intunecat never underestimated the powers of spirits, especially Mari.

The next day, Yemaya, Dakota, and Andrei met with Kenyon and several of the townspeople. The girl's body had been taken to her family and prepared for burial.

"They fear drac has returned," Kenyon said anxiously, glancing at several of his neighbors.

"It may be true, Kenyon," Yemaya warned, remembering her earlier conversation with Dakota. Over breakfast, Dakota described the dream and the warning about Intunecat, especially the information on the false merging. Yemaya was stunned that she had been fooled so easily. It was unsettling to think anything could get past her defenses. If not for Dakota and Regina...she didn't even want to think about the ramifications.

"How do we fight the drac, Ms. Lysanne?"

"You don't. My people and I will handle it. You tell your people to stay inside at night. Never travel alone and keep an eye out for strangers. Let me know of anyone or anything unusual or suspicious. The wolves will patrol the forests and town perimeter until this is over with."

The wolves and the townspeople had coexisted peacefully for over a millennium. Rarely did they come to the village. Kenyon knew it was a bad omen when the mistress sent the wolves.

Over breakfast, the man listened to the gossip. The girl had been found and the villagers were frightened. The elders had met with Lysanne earlier and had instructed everyone to stay inside after nightfall.

"Shit," he muttered. "How am I going to find another girl?"

"When the time is right, I will give one to you," the voice answered. "I already have her picked out. You will like this one. She'll be a challenge, but you're up to it."

The man smiled, already anticipating his next fantasy.

"When?" he asked.

"Soon, very soon. Be patient."

Three days passed without incident. Some hoped the killer would just move on. The man was getting impatient. Yemaya and Dakota could only wait for him to reappear. Andrei and the men spent several days searching the forests for any sign of the killer. The wolves caught a faint scent of something but nothing definable. Everyone was frustrated, knowing he was still out there waiting for his next victim.

"The child is being buried today," Yemaya reminded, more for something to say than anything else.

"I know. I promised her family I would visit them after the funeral. It'll keep me busy while you meet with the town elders," Dakota said.

"The service is at two, later than I would like, but there are friends and family coming from distant villages. Make sure you stay with them afterward until Andrei or I pick you up."

"Yes, Mom," Dakota teased.

Yemaya arched her brow and smirked.

"Bet your mom never made you feel like I do."

"Good Lord I hope not," Dakota laughed. "What an awful thought."

Yemaya chuckled at the disgusted look on Dakota's face.

"Well, I guess we need to get a move on it."

Andrei was waiting by the drawbridge. Opening the door for Dakota, he tipped his hat and smiled.

"Evening Ms. Devereaux, mistress."

"Hi, Andrei. Thanks," Dakota said.

"Thanks, Andrei," Yemaya added.

Thirty minutes later, Dakota was dropped off at the small church on the outskirts of town. Several hundred people had already arrived. Even though it was chilly, the ceremony was held outside to accommodate the huge congregation of mourners.

As the mistress's companion, she was offered a seat in the front row but chose to sit farther back. Yemaya had already sent her condolences with an explanation she needed to meet with the elders to see if any new information was available.

The services lasted about an hour before the coffin was carried to the cemetery and lowered into the grave. Another small ceremony was performed at the grave site and everyone dispersed, anxious to get home before the sun set.

Dakota was invited to accompany the girl's family home. The house was warmed by a central fireplace. A large iron pot containing mutton stew was hanging over the flames. Warm bread sat on a platter on the large wooden table in the kitchen area.

The girl's mother gestured for Dakota to sit. The rest of the family sat around the table, each taking a turn at ladling soup into a bowl and taking a chunk of broken bread.

"It's time," the voice said. "You must hurry if you want the woman."

The man was almost asleep when the voice woke him. Jumping up, he grinned.

"About time," he said excitedly. "Where is she?"

"She is at the home of the girl's family. You must be patient, though. It won't be easy to get her to leave the house by herself. I'll help, but you must do exactly what I say and be quick."

"I will. Whatever you say." His excitement grew. His needs were great now.

"She'll fight you if you hesitate. If you fail, you'll be caught, and I won't be able to help you. You'll be on your own. Do you understand?"

"Sure."

The voice gave him instructions. Nodding, he put on his jacket and left for the girl's home.

Yemaya sat with several elders discussing the details of the investigations by the local police force and her people. Little information was available. Several strangers were in the neighborhood. Most had either family connections or friends. A few businessmen were visiting the wineries trying to finalize deals. The rest seemed to be migrants, backpackers, or sightseers. None of them acted unusual.

Scanning the names, Yemaya eliminated the ones least likely to be the killer. Friends or family members were the first. Several had arrived after the killing, or their time could be accounted for by someone else. By the time she was done, only three people seemed to have either shaky alibis or none at all.

"I want these three followed at all times," Yemaya ordered. "And I want background checks on them. Check the motel and backpacker inn records on these two. This one," she said, tapping her finger on his file, "talk with Mr. Romalty at the winery. See if he can tell you any more about when he arrived and where he is staying. If Romalty is still out of town, ask his wife. She knows everything that happens in the vineyards."

"Yes, mistress," Kenyon replied. "I'll send men out immediately."

"Good. Now what else is there to discuss? We might as well get any business done now so we do not have to meet tomorrow."

Yemaya was anxious to get back to Dakota, but she didn't want to attend the funeral. It was bad enough sharing everyone's sorrow, but for her, it was extremely painful. Her unique abilities were a blessing and a curse. Such sorrow in so many people overwhelmed her senses, pounding on the door to her emotions like a battering ram. Twice she had endured the agony and she swore never again.

Several hours later, she looked at her watch and decided it was time to pick up Dakota and head home. Dismissing the group, she called Andrei, who was at his sister's house about twenty minutes away.

Dakota listened to the family as they talked about the services and all the people who had attended the funeral. They were honored by her presence as the special representative of their mistress. She assured them it was her honor and thanked them for their hospitality.

A banging on the door interrupted the conversation. When the daughter opened the door, a young man excused himself, pushed past the girl, and rushed in. Seeing Dakota, he hurried to her and bowed.

"Please forgive, Ms. Devereaux," he apologized. "The mistress sent me to you. There was acci–accident. Mistress hurt. You go to her, yes?"

Dakota jumped up and grabbed her coat.

"Where is she?" she demanded, her voice shaking.

"Close. She close! We go now," he stated, his eyes lowered respectfully, his voice surprisingly low. Had Dakota looked closely at his young face, she would have seen black eyes gleaming unnaturally.

"Yes, we go now."

"Ms. Devereaux," the girl's father said, "I will go with you. You mustn't go out alone."

"She hurt bad, miss. But we wait if you want."

"No, we're going now," she ordered. "I'm not alone. This young man will keep me company. Please call the estate and tell Maria to send another car immediately. Where exactly is she?" she asked the young man.

Giving her the names of an intersection about six blocks away, he rushed to the door and stepped outside.

"Tell her we'll be at that location," Dakota said.

Dakota hurried after the young man. It was an effort to keep up as he moved quickly through the deserted streets. For a moment, she lost sight of him when he stepped around a corner. As she rounded the corner, she caught a quick glimpse of a fist before the pain exploded in her jaw, knocking her unconscious.

The young man stood looking at the woman's crumpled body lying on the ground.

"Did I not tell you she was beautiful?" the voice asked.

"Yes," the man replied. "Very beautiful."

"Take her to the meadow and be quick," the voice commanded. "You may not kill her till I tell you to, but she is yours to enjoy."

The man stooped to pick up the limp form. When he straightened, the boy had vanished.

"We're going to have some fun," the man promised. He continued talking to the unconscious woman as he walked into the woods unaware he was being watched. Cold golden-flecked serpentine eyes opened slowly when he walked past a fallen tree. Slowly, the long slender body reluctantly uncoiled. It slithered across the ground several feet behind the intruder.

Andrei was about fifteen minutes away from Yemaya when she felt the pain. Something was horribly wrong. Placing her palms against her temples, she pressed hard.

"You musssstt hurrry," Sarpe hissed, her silky soft voice easing through Yemaya's pain. "My kin is following the human. He has your life mate."

"Where are they, Sarpe?"

"In the foresssst. He carries her toward the sssame placcce as before. I will let the others know."

"Thank you," Yemaya said gratefully. It would be at least forty-five minutes before she and Andrei could reach the edge of the forest.

Ursa felt helpless. Her kin were hibernating. Waking them would take too long to help the mortal.

"What can we do?" she grumbled angrily. "Mine are unable to do anything now. They sleep too deeply to wake up." She flexed her paws helplessly.

"Ursa, be calm. Let me think," Arbora said firmly. "Sarpe's kin follows the Dark One's servant. She will do what she can. I'll try to locate Intunecat, and you must get Mari and Maopa. It is imperative they come. Now go, my love," she whispered, embracing the bear spirit.

Arbora knew it would be difficult to find the Dark One. Nighttime in the woods made everything dark. Shadows were long and plentiful, and they moved as swiftly as the moon across the black skies.

It was fortunate Sarpe's kin was still able to move. The cold nights often made them sluggish, and they were usually reluctant to leave their warm burrows. Sarpe had to be supplementing their energies with her own. How long she could continue, though, was questionable. It was difficult to maintain a connection between the spirit and mortal worlds. She would pay dearly for her efforts.

. Ursa growled and grumbled. Ladyhawk felt the disturbance. Soaring from her high perch, she landed on the bear spirit's broad shoulder.

"So it begins," she declared.

"I must get to Mari and Maopa quickly."

"Merge with me, Ursa. With your help, we can get there faster than either of us alone."

Ursa had never merged with anyone other than Arbora. She hesitated.

"It's okay," Arbora's voice assured her. "I understand."

Once together, Ladyhawk streaked toward Mari's domain. By the time she arrived, the water and human spirits were already discussing the situation.

"Vyushir has sent the wolves to the meadow to await the human. I've told her to tell them to do nothing until Yemaya arrives. He will kill Dakota if he suspects anything is wrong," Mari said.

"That be so. We must let the magic woman deal with him. She be the only one who kin get inside his head ta fight the darkness."

"She will need our help," Ladyhawk said.

"We must hurry."

The three spirits vanished simultaneously.

Chapter Eighteen

As the man wound through the trees carrying his prize, he noticed the wind starting to gust. An owl hooted nearby, causing him to jump. In the distance, a wolf's howl drowned out the high screech of a raptor. Soon, tree limbs started falling around him. Apparently, a storm was brewing, making the animals uneasy, causing them to stir and voice their discomfort.

He shivered, cold and uneasy. Where was the quiet like the time before? Why wasn't the voice here to reassure him? The meadow was still an hour away. His pace quickened.

Yemaya jumped from the Hummer and ran into the woods. Andrei would bring some men and follow her. Regina and Voinic waited impatiently at the forest edge. When their mistress arrived, they positioned themselves on each side of her before leading the way. They were concerned that Simtire might do something rash to save Dakota. She too had felt the attack when it occurred. Even her allegiance to Regina would not stop her from rushing off to the meadow. Only after Voinic shouldered her to the ground did she calm down. No amount of persuasion would stop her from helping Dakota, but she acknowledged the alpha pair's orders to do nothing until Yemaya arrived unless Dakota was in imminent danger.

"Simtire."

Startled, Simtire slowed to a trot, looking all around. This voice was not that of her pack, but it demanded her attention.

"Simtire, I am Vyushir."

"Vyushir," she growled in awe.

"I know you want to help your mistress, but if you attack the human, he will kill her and you. If you want to help her, you must be patient. *The* mistress comes. She must handle this."

"I won't let my mistress be harmed. I will die before that happens," the young female wolf declared.

"And she will die if you become impatient. You must wait," Vyushir ordered.

"I will wait for a while, Vyushir."

"That's all I ask of you," the wolf spirit answered. "Now go and wait."

Simtire lay in the shadows behind a dead tree trunk. She could smell the man and the scent of her mistress. Lips curling, she felt her muscles tighten. It would only take a moment for her to reach him and rip out his throat.

"No," a voice hissed to her left. Startled she looked around, her eyes settling on a huge orange and black snake. "You will ssssstay as you promisssed," Sarpe ordered, her eyes coal black and deadly, her head swaying slowly back and forth. "The missstresssss is near. Patienccce, youngsssster. Your time will come ssssoon enough."

Simtire reluctantly relaxed and settled down to watch. Sarpe nodded approvingly and lowered her head.

"I will move clossssser. If your missstresssss needs our help, you will know. We won't allow her to be sssseriousssly harmed," the snake spirit promised as she slithered through the grass.

The man finally made it to the meadow. His heart pounded furiously from fear and the exertion of carrying the unconscious woman. Something was wrong. The voice wasn't around. The night was alive with sounds and shadows. He laid Dakota on the grass, straightening her body and positioning it as if she were sleeping. The blow to her jaw must have been harder than he realized. She should have been awake by now. There was no way he could continue if she wasn't awake.

Dakota felt like she was on a boat, swaying back and forth. Disoriented, she struggled to open her eyes.

"Sleep, Dakota."

The voice was low, soft, seductive. Warm spectral fingers stroked her brow, easing the pain and confusion.

"Yemaya will be here soon, little one," the hypnotic voice promised. "I can't let you awaken yet."

Dakota relaxed, settling into a deep slumber.

Intunecat stormed through the darkness, trying to reach the man's mind. Somehow the spirits had managed to separate the link between him and the human. The only way he could reach the man was to take on a human form. Unfortunately, once he had assumed that shape, he became vulnerable. It was a chance he had to take. Changing again into the young man, he materialized at the edge of the forest. The man was standing over the woman, looking around in fear. Stepping into the meadow, he called out.

"Why do you hesitate?" he demanded.

"Where have you been? Something's wrong. The noises. The trees. Everything is moving now," the man yelled, frustrated and afraid.

"They are only noises. If you don't want to take your pleasure now, then do as I've instructed and kill her," Intunecat ordered. "Others will be here soon."

The man looked down at the still form. Pulling the knife from his belt, he stared at its reflection in the moonlight.

"But she's not awake. I can't kill her till she wakes up. She has to know I'm not going to hurt her," he explained illogically.

"Do as I say," the voice warned. "Kill her."

Sighing, the man started to kneel when a large orange and black snake slid over the woman's chest, coiling lazily across her torso. Screaming, the man jumped back as the snake turned black unblinking eyes in his direction. A forked tongue slipped between closed lips, tasting the air.

"Jesus fucking Christ," the man cursed, stumbling backward. "Where'd that come from?"

"It's harmless," the voice said. "You can kill it with your knife. You must kill it and the woman. I'll help you as I did before. Remember how you killed the wolf. This snake can't harm you."

The man's hand trembled. Barely able to hold the knife, he looked at the young man standing near the forest, then back at the woman and the snake.

"You...you kill the snake," he stammered, holding the knife out as an offering to the other man. "You kill it and I'll take care of the girl."

Intunecat realized he was getting nowhere. Cursing, he walked over and looked at the knife.

"So, Sarpe, we meet as mortals," he declared. "And so you will die."

"If it is my dessstiny, sssso be it."

A low growl from behind Intunecat caught his attention. A young wolf was slowly moving in his direction, her hackles raised, lips curled, and fangs bared.

"It would sssseeem we have company," Sarpe hissed, her head moving back and forth. "Who will you try to kill firsssst?"

"The wolf is no threat to me," Intunecat answered. "Just as you are not one. I may be in human form, but I'm immortal. I am older than time. You spirits foolishly think a mortal wolf pup and a spirit—even one as old as you—can defeat me so easily."

"No," Sarpe said. "Alone I'm no match for you."

Intunecat smiled, his eyes gleaming brightly.

"But with our help, it won't be so easy," Mari interrupted as she materialized between him and Sarpe.

"That be the truth," the elder Dakota agreed, appearing with Ladyhawk on her shoulder. The hawk spirit nodded without breaking eye contact with the Dark One.

Intunecat laughed.

"So the Council of Seven has convened," he sneered. "Where are the others? Hiding?"

"They are here," Mari replied. Arbora and Ursa shimmered into existence near Dakota. Vyushir appeared next to Simtire, her eyes flashing angrily.

"You killed one of mine," she growled at the man. "The debt must be paid."

The man was terrified by the appearance of the spirits. The voice promised to help him, but there were so many of them. He crossed himself and began praying as he backed away from the group.

"Prayers won't help you," a cold, angry voice whispered from behind. Turning quickly, he searched for the source.

"Where are you?" he demanded, fear giving him a small degree of courage.

"I'm here," the voice replied. "Beside you."

He turned around but saw nothing.

"I don't see you. Show yourself," he yelled, holding the knife out defensively.

Yemaya stood behind the man, quietly contemplating what she was going to do with him. He had tortured and killed the young woman, killed the wolf pup, and injured her lover. Inside, she seethed. Vengeance would be sweet, she thought.

"He is sick," her lover's voice murmured softly, interrupting her thoughts. "Vengeance is never as good as we imagine."

"He killed the girl and the wolf, and he hurt you," Yemaya mentally raged.

"Then he should be punished," Dakota reasoned. "But not by you, my love."

"A debt must be repaid. It is our way. Vyushir demands justice. I cannot just let the townspeople try him." She tried to make Dakota realize the importance of the pact between her and the wolves.

"Then it's up to you to figure out a way to satisfy the debt and give him justice," Dakota rationalized. "You must do this, Yemaya. Vengeance will give the Dark One what he wants—you—and I can't allow that. I'll die first."

The entire mental conversation took only seconds. Yemaya sighed, looking at the others. At the moment, they were distracting Intunecat. She knew she needed to do something quickly.

Searching his mind, she pried into the darkest corners looking for an answer, the seeds of his insanity. As a child, he had been damaged by his abusive father. Faint memories of a mother who sacrificed herself to protect him from his dad's terrifying temper still remained, tucked deeply away in a small secluded spot.

Reaching in, she grabbed the memories and pulled them out, weaving each event through his conscience like fine needlework. The boy had loved his mother, but she was too weak to protect him—a weakness he blamed her for. After years of beatings and humiliation, his father finally succeeded in destroying his love for his mother.

"She loved you, you know," Yemaya spoke, her voice gentle, calming.

"She was weak," the man answered, suddenly thinking of his mother.

"She was strong," Yemaya countered. "She endured your father's beatings and remained silent so you wouldn't be harmed."

"No! I heard her! She begged him to stop. She never fought him," the man said, shaking his head angrily.

"If she had resisted, he would have killed her. Then he would have focused on you. She loved you so much, she endured as long as she could to keep you safe, even after she realized you had become like him."

Tears streamed down the man's face but still he denied the truth. His father always told him women were weak. His mother proved it. Women were meant to serve and pleasure men.

"You remember the day your mother died?" Yemaya continued.

The man nodded, closing his eyes. His father had just lost his job. He started drinking after he came home. His mother did her best to avoid him, which angered him further, sending him into a rage.

"She took your hand and begged for your forgiveness. What were her dying words? Du'dera, Dalnos, Mie Sedre."

Yemaya nudged the memory forward. He was seventeen. His father had finally gone too far. In his drunken fervor, he threw her to the floor and kicked her stomach until he passed out.

She suffered internal injuries so severe nothing could be done to save her. He remembered kneeling next to her as she lay on the living room floor, bruised and bleeding. She carefully took his hand, running her thumb over the palm, her eyes wet with tears and slightly glazed as death closed in.

"I'm so sorry, Dalnos, my child. Remember, I always loved you. I will always love you." And she died.

He had stared at the hand that still held his, even in death. His mother had deserted him. Just like that. He dropped the hand, stood, and walked away, never looking back. He stole some money from his father's wallet, packed a few items, and left.

"She never left. See, she's here, Dalnos," Yemaya whispered.

Dalnos opened his eyes. Before him stood his mother, her face young and beautiful. There were no bruises, no scars. Only a warm smile as she held out her arms, her hands motioning him forward.

"Mama?" Dalnos cried, tears streaming down his cheeks. "Is that you, mama?"

"Mie Sedre," she replied, her voice warm and loving. Dalnos rushed forward, wrapping his arms around her waist, leaning into her warm embrace. Resting his cheek on her breast, he sobbed.

"Mama, I missed you so much. I was so alone when you left," he mumbled against her chest.

"I know, but I never left you. I've always been here," his mother whispered, her cheek pressed against his hair. "You just couldn't hear me."

Dalnos nodded.

"I heard so many voices, mama. They kept whispering to me. Telling me to do horrible things. I guess they drowned you out, huh?" he asked, trying to remember if he might have missed hers somehow.

"I guess so, son. But you don't hear them now, do you?"

"No, mama, only you," he replied happily.

"Then you will only hear mine from now on. The others won't bother you anymore, I promise. Do you believe me?"

"Yes, mama." Dalnos smiled childlike.

"We must go now. Others are coming and you have to go with them," his mother explained.

"I'm afraid. They want to hurt me," he whimpered. "I hurt one of them." For the first time, he felt remorse.

"I know, my son. I'll be with you. They won't hurt you, I promise." Putting her arm around him, the two walked toward the town, the man's head bent slightly forward, his arms hanging limply.

Yemaya watched the man walk away lost in the memories of his mother. Vyushir growled when he passed her but didn't attack. Yemaya had honored her request for the blood debt a few weeks back. She would allow this human to live. Yemaya tipped her head, acknowledging the gift, then turned to the others.

Since his link had been severed earlier, Intunecat wasn't sure what had transpired between Yemaya and the man, but he knew she had somehow overcome his darkness. As much as he wanted her for himself, he grudgingly admired her accomplishment. Maybe the spirits had helped her or perhaps her lover, or she could be more powerful than he imagined. There would be other times to find out.

Once Yemaya arrived, the spirits remained silent. The battle was hers and Dakota's to win or lose. They had merely delayed the Dark One long enough for Dakota to help Yemaya gain control of her emotions.

Yemaya approached Intunecat, stopping a few feet away. Her gaze slowly assessed the human form in front of her.

"You are the Dark One," she said softly, thinking how human he looked.

"Yes." His voice was deep and pleasant but emotionless.

"Why?" she asked, knowing he understood the many questions behind the one word.

"Why did I have the girl killed? She was my path to you. Why the man? He was the tool, and he was mad. That made him easy. Why did I go after your life mate? Because she is your weakness and your strength," he replied casually.

"Why me?"

"You are the key to my desires," he answered truthfully. "Once I possess you, I will possess this world and the spirit world. It's not complicated."

"Your desires," she repeated. "Your desires are so important you would do something this terrible to achieve them?"

"You judge me unfairly. Come with me to my world and you will understand," he offered.

"Never."

Intunecat shrugged.

"Never is a long time. You ask me about my desires. The answer lies in my world. Only there will you find and understand my whys."

"As I said before—never."

"So be it. Now I must ask. What did you do to him? I've never lost one of mine before."

"Nothing," Yemaya replied. "He simply remembered a moment in time before he became what he is now. His life has been a journey of misery. Why would he not choose to live in the happiness of his past rather than the pain of the present?" she asked philosophically.

"If you say so. But I think there is more to it than that."

Yemaya shrugged.

"Think what you want. You would have to live in my world to understand," she countered sarcastically.

Realizing there was nothing further to gain, Intunecat decided it was time to leave.

"This is the second time you've thwarted me. I don't take defeat lightly. We will meet again and again until you make the journey to my world. It's your destiny," he said matter-of-factly.

While Yemaya was confronting the Dark One, Mari woke Dakota from her deep slumber. She listened quietly to the exchange between Yemaya and Intunecat. Even asleep, she had been aware of the events around her. She had reached out to her lover to soothe the anger raging inside. Once Yemaya calmed down, she pulled back but didn't withdraw.

Intunecat watched the small mortal as she walked over to Yemaya and wrapped her arm around the taller woman's waist.

"*We* make our destiny, not you," Dakota answered, interrupting the conversation. "Yemaya will never be yours. She's mine, she'll always be mine. I may not have the powers you or Yemaya or the others have, but I love her, and that gives me the strength to defeat you anytime."

Yemaya smirked. Dakota certainly was a feisty one. To take on the Dark One may be unwise, but it revealed the full extent of Dakota's love for her.

Intunecat smiled, genuinely amused at the human's audacity. He admired her courage and her spirit. Time was on his side, so he had no doubts about Yemaya's future with him, but the battle among him, the spirits, and the two mortals would end his boredom for a while.

"We will see, little one. Until then, enjoy the quiet times," he advised sincerely and vanished, leaving the two confused.

"He really isn't evil," Mari explained after Intunecat's departure. "His suffering is unimaginable. He endures a world of darkness filled with a great loneliness. Before meeting Maopa, I too knew such loneliness. I wouldn't wish it on anyone," she said sadly.

"That be the truth, chillins. I feels sorry fer him."

The other spirits nodded in agreement.

"How do we thank all of you?" Yemaya asked, refusing to empathize with the spirit who had caused her so much trouble.

"Ya doesn't," the elder Dakota chuckled. "We had a lot of fun and gots to knowed each other a lot better. Made some new friends, we did. Why I may even learn Mari a few things she taint never knowed. After all, she taint never been mortal, liken usens, 'bout time she learned a thang or two 'bout what we does when we gets aroused," she said, her eyes twinkling mischievously.

"Maopa, hush," Mari ordered, her pale silver cheeks suddenly turning a light shade of pink. "You talk way too much. Let's leave these two so they can go home and rest. I'm sure they're tired."

Laughing, Grandma Dakota winked at her granddaughter and life mate, then vanished with Ladyhawk. Mari smiled mischievously and quickly followed. Ursa and Arbora returned to the forest, talking quietly about the evening's events, leaving only Sarpe and Vyushir.

"Sarpe, how do I thank you for protecting Dakota? You would have died if the man had attacked you with the knife."

"I too undersssstand lonelinessss. You have sssssomeone. She is a precccccious gift. One day, I hope to meet ssssomeone I can share my thoughtssss with," Sarpe explained. "I could do nothing lesssss."

"Then I too hope you find someone and soon. Your kin are as my own now and will be protected by me and mine from this moment on," Yemaya promised, creating a new alliance between Carpi and serpent. Sarpe bowed her head, accepting the pact.

"Vyushir, I am in your debt, too. You also helped to protect Dakota until I arrived. The Lysannes will never be able to repay you."

"The debt was paid when you saved Simtire. The alliance stands strong as it always has and always will," Vyushir said graciously. "Now I must take this young wolf pup back to her den. She needs a few lessons in obedience and patience. Please tell your life mate she will have to do without her for a few days."

Vyushir turned to Sarpe.

"You took many chances, my friend. Simtire was frightened when she saw such a large snake, but she isn't a coward. She could have attacked and harmed you." The wolf spirit was greatly concerned over the thought of the serpent spirit being hurt or killed.

"The wolf is young, but she is wise. I was never in danger from her." Sarpe tried to ease Vyushir's concern.

"Well, perhaps you would like to accompany us. I'm sure your thoughts would be beneficial in lessons on obedience," she growled, slewing a glance at Simtire.

"It would be my pleasure," Sarpe hissed, uncoiling her long body.

Once Sarpe, Simtire, and Vyushir were gone, Yemaya and Dakota headed home. Regina loped ahead to make sure everything was okay. Voinic went in search of Andrei and the others to forewarn them about the man. They had found him walking absentmindedly through the forests talking quietly to himself.

When he saw them, he smiled childlike and waved. His mother hadn't lied. She had stayed with him, encouraging him to be brave and to trust the big man leading the group. Andrei put his arm around Dalnos's shoulder. For the first time in his life, Dalnos was truly happy and at peace with himself. The townspeople followed closely behind, confused but unwilling to question or challenge the mistress's most trusted employee.

Chapter Nineteen

Yemaya and Dakota snuggled under the blankets. Maria had sent the car to pick them up. A hot meal was waiting for them in the study. Afterward, she shooed them off to bed. A warm bath and two hours of gentle lovemaking later, they felt relaxed enough to talk about the earlier events.

"I think I will have to keep you under lock and key," Yemaya teased.

"In your dreams," Dakota responded, slapping her lover's arm. "You're the one always getting into trouble. If I didn't keep coming to your rescue, you'd be totally in the dark about what's going on around you."

"That is a terrible pun," Yemaya groaned. "Seriously, though, how is your head? You cannot keep taking blows like that."

"It's fine, honestly, and I don't plan on getting any more," she joked. "Has your life always been this interesting?"

"I always thought it was somewhat interesting, but nothing like this. Things started happening when you entered it."

"Same here. My life was pretty boring till I met you," she replied. "Do you think Mari and Grams are an item now?"

"I would say they are well on their way. I even got the impression Sarpe and Vyushir might find something in common to share."

"I owe those two a lot, Sarpe especially. I'll never look at snakes the same way again," Dakota commented. "What about Ladyhawk? She seems to have no one."

"I do not know, love. She seems contented with Grandma Dakota. Maybe that is enough for her."

"Maybe," Dakota agreed. "But I hope not. Ladyhawk should have someone of her own. Threesome's never work."

"Well, I guess we will just have to keep an eye out for a good looking spirit then," Yemaya suggested, raising an eyebrow.

Dakota remained quiet for a moment, then decided to change the subject.

"What's going to happen to Dalnos? I know he's a killer, but I can't help but feel sad because of his childhood."

"I know. Had you not stopped me, I would have killed him for what he did to the girl, the wolf, and especially you." Yemaya's voice was suddenly cold and emotionless.

"But you didn't."

"No, once I calmed down, I was able to think more clearly. When I learned about his childhood and why he was so flawed, I felt sorry for him. How many people are destroyed by someone they love? It is a sobering lesson. Anyway, the past is done. I am not sure what the voices were that he heard, other than Intunecat's. Maybe just his insanity crying out. After all these years, though, he needed someone to talk to and to listen to. I gave him back his mother."

"Thank you for that," Dakota said, stroking Yemaya's arm absentmindedly. "Is there anything else you'd like to tell me?" she smirked.

Laughing, the two snuggled deeper and quickly fell asleep.

For the first time in eons, Intunecat didn't feel the loneliness. His encounter with the spirits and the two mortals had temporarily filled the emptiness inside of him. He laughed softly to himself. Tonight the mortal world was safe.

Ironically, they would never know. Their fears were still alive and well.

Sonny read the report and threw it on the desk. Someone definitely was interested in Yemaya's background. Several efforts had been made to access her records with Immigration and the IRS, not to mention the FBI, CIA, and Secret Service. His sources revealed a systematic hacker attack on multiple computers pertaining to her and her brother. Whoever the person was, he or she was good, very good.

Unfortunately for them, there was nothing of value or interest in the records. Sealing them had been more a formality than a necessity. The Lysannes were extremely efficient at minimizing information about themselves to government entities. He didn't know what or who they knew, but it was obvious they had powerful inside connections on the highest levels. Picking up the phone, he dialed Yemaya's number, dreading having to relay the news to her. Interrupting her much-needed vacation was a bitch, but she needed to get back to the States quickly.

"Allo. Lysanne k'ena."

"Maria? This is Sonny. Is Ms. Lysanne in?"

"Ah, Mr. Marino. How are you?"

"Fine, Maria. How are you and Andrei doing?"

"Everything okay here. The mistress and Ms. Devereaux are resting. Lots of things happening here," she confided.

"Really. Like what?"

"Better if Ms. Lysanne tell you. I talk too much. I'll get her. Nice to hear from you, Mr. Marino."

Sonny heard a click as the phone was put down on a table. Looking out the window, he noticed a few flakes of snow falling.

Damn, he thought. *It's going to be an early winter.*

His thoughts were interrupted by the low, husky voice of Yemaya.

"Good morning, Sonny."

Sonny shivered. There was an eerie seductiveness about her voice. It caressed, soothed, and calmed his thoughts, reminding him of a warm breeze blowing serenely over a cool body of water. At the same time, he could feel his heartbeat increasing. He had known her for years. Time didn't diminish its effect.

"Good evening, Yemaya. Sorry to intrude on your vacation."

"No problem. For you, anything," she teased.

"I wish," Sonny replied half joking.

"What can I do for you?" Yemaya asked, chuckling quietly.

"I just received the report on the Charleston episode. The platform definitely was sabotaged. We think it was by a repairman called in to do some work on the circulation pumps, and we think the pumps were vandalized to get him there."

"Do we know who the repairman was or anything about his company?"

"That's the problem. The curator gave us the name, but it appears to be a non-working number. The phone company says the number is one of those prepaid phones. No way to track it."

"Where did the curator get the name then?"

"From his secretary, but she says it was in her rollerdecks file. She inherited the file from the previous employee about five years ago. We contacted the former secretary, and she never heard of the company."

"All this leads us to what?"

"A dead end at the moment. Obviously, there are some very influential people behind this. Someone has been trying to hack your records from several government agencies. They didn't get much, but the fact they could actually access your records is enough to show this isn't just a fan or overly curious reporter."

"You may be right. I suppose I should cut this trip short and head back to the States. Let me talk with Dakota. I can get with you about the arrangements."

"I really don't think that's necessary at the moment. Go ahead and enjoy the time off. I'll call you if you need to change things. Speaking of Ms. Devereaux, how is she doing? Is she anything like her picture?" Sonny teased.

"Better, much better. If you are a good boy, I might even introduce you to her," Yemaya smirked.

"Boy? Damn, Yemaya, I'm forty-nine years old, long past the boy stage," Sonny chuckled. "I'd love to meet the woman who caught your eye, though."

"Sure. Listen, I have to take care of some business here. Call me if you find anything out."

"Will do. I'll talk to you in a few days. Take care and be careful."

"Always. Thanks, Sonny."

Yemaya placed the phone in the receiver and turned to Dakota, who was sipping hot cocoa made from Belgium chocolate.

"Trouble?"

"Not really sure. Seems someone besides you has been digging into my personal life."

"I would imagine this happens a lot. What makes this time so different?"

"This time, my records have been hacked at several U.S. government agencies. The platform was definitely tampered with by a repairman who works for a company that does not exist and had a prepaid phone that cannot be traced."

"I guess that would make it a little more unusual. Why am I not surprised?" Dakota commented. "Is your life always like this?"

"Only since I met you, love," Yemaya smirked. "Before I was just a simple person, leading a boring life traveling all over the world trying to make a living."

Yemaya actually batted her eyelashes, giving Dakota an exaggerated innocent look.

Dakota snorted as chocolate bubbled from her nose. Grabbing a napkin, she coughed a couple of times and wiped her face.

"Paleeeze."

Placing her right hand over her heart, Yemaya sighed deeply. "You doubt me. I fear you have wounded me deeply, my love."

"Yeah, yeah," Dakota chuckled. "You'll survive."

"Now that is what I call sympathy," Yemaya countered, glancing at her watch. "I guess we need to get a move on it. We leave Thursday, which means packing and going into town to make sure everything is okay. Raidon will be back by then, but I want to check on the girl's family and Dalnos."

"What are they going to do with him?"

"Probably put him on trial. He will be found guilty, of course. Our system is not as complicated as yours, so everything moves quickly here."

"Will he be executed?"

"No, I talked with Kenyon. When he is found guilty, he will be taken to a special hospital and confined there for the rest of his life."

"When he's found guilty? Doesn't sound like he's going to get a fair trial if he's already been pronounced guilty."

"Dakota, he *is* guilty. That is what matters first to us. We take into consideration the circumstances when we pronounce the sentence, but we do not complicate the issue with confusing jargon, technicalities, or superfluous evidence. Like I said, our system is different."

"I'm glad he won't be killed. I've always hated the death penalty."

"Me too, but sometimes it is a necessary evil. Perhaps because of our history, we accept it as the final solution if nothing else works. Fortunately, we rarely have to exercise that option."

"I don't think I could ever accept it as an alternative."

"I am glad. I hope you never change. Now I need to take care of some business in town. I should be back in a few hours."

"Stay out of trouble, will you?" Dakota teased.

Ruffling Dakota's hair, Yemaya leaned down and gave her a quick kiss.

"Yes, dear."

Dalnos sat in the corner of his cell talking quietly with the voice of his mother. Yemaya's instructions to Kenyon were very specific. The man was to be treated like a sick child. It was their responsibility to make sure he was fed, clothed, and cleaned and he was not to be abused in any way. Some of the men were angry about this. One of their children had been horribly abused, tortured, then murdered. It was an abomination to treat the killer so kindly. Justice demanded he be executed for his crimes.

During the trip into town, Yemaya gave Andrei additional instructions about Dalnos and the trial. Because he couldn't defend himself, she had hired a local attorney to represent him. Granted it was a formality, but Yemaya still believed he was entitled to a defense.

"It seems a waste to have a trial, mistress," Andrei said.

"I know, but he is unable to defend himself, so we have to do it for him. It is the right thing to do."

"In the old days, he would have been beheaded and done with."

"We have progressed beyond the old days. Supposedly, we are more civilized, although sometimes I wonder."

"As do I, mistress. By the way, Sasha phoned me yesterday."

"How is she?" Yemaya asked. She knew Andrei and his cousin were extremely close. Now that the young woman was going to the university in the States, he often worried about her.

"She's fine. She said she's going to take a trip with some girlfriends. Maybe the next time you're there you will visit her."

"I would like that very much. Tell her I said hello."

"I will. Thank you," Andrei said, grateful for her interest.

When Yemaya and Andrei arrived at the local jail, several men were gathered outside. Two seemed to be having a heated argument.

"He's a murderer. Since when do we treat murderers this way?" a tall bearded man demanded.

"Since the mistress ordered it," the smaller one responded, blocking the entranceway.

"She isn't our queen to order us about like peons. I am no servitor. I am a man," he shouted, thumping his chest with his fist. "I say what is or what isn't."

"Hush, Alto. She's the mistress."

Alto spit on the ground. "She isn't my mistress. My mistress would be at home warming my bed at night or doing my cooking and laundry. She's only a woman with money and a name."

The smaller man suddenly backed away from the taller villager. Crossing himself, he muttered a prayer, refusing to look up.

"Bresnak, you're a coward," Alto said disgustedly.

"Are you unhappy about something, Alto?" Yemaya murmured, her voice low and barely audible.

Alto jumped and spun around, almost losing his balance. Before him stood the object of his discussion, her eyes a frosty blue. Straightening to his full height, he stared down at Yemaya, his upper lip curled in a sneer.

"Yes, I say we take the murderer and do to him what he did to the girl."

"I see. And I suppose you will be the one to hand out this punishment?" she asked coldly.

"If no one else has the balls, I do," Alto stated arrogantly.

"Fine. Then do it," Yemaya ordered.

"Huh?"

"You heard me, kill him."

Turning to Georgio, she ordered him to get Dalnos. When he returned with the man, she stepped close to Alto and motioned toward the prisoner.

"He is yours."

Alto hesitated. This wasn't what he expected. Looking around, he saw a crowd had gathered to listen.

"Now? How am I to kill him? I need a weapon," he bluffed.

"No weapon. You say you are a man. Use your hands. He is a child now. He will offer no resistance. All you have to do is wrap your fingers around his neck and squeeze. Be the man you claim to be, Alto, if that is your idea of one," Yemaya snarled.

Several members in the crowd gasped. Why was the mistress doing this? Had she changed her mind? Couldn't Alto see this one was sick?

Alto glanced down at his hands. He'd never killed anyone. The thought of choking someone, even a person like Dalnos, frightened him.

"I...I...can't kill him like this," he said. "It's the law's responsibility to do it." He tried to regain his composure.

"No, Alto. You demand justice, his execution. You have judged and sentenced him already. That just leaves killing him. The others wait for you to carry out the justice you demanded."

Alto looked around. No one said anything.

"I have work to do," Alto declared, changing the subject. "I don't have time for this. This is for the law to decide."

Turning, he stalked off muttering to himself.

Yemaya looked at the remaining men.

"Anyone else?"

Looking sheepish, the others decided they had more important matters to tend to.

Yemaya shook her head and motioned for Andrei to take Dalnos back to his cell.

The man was oblivious to the events around him. His world was now his mother, and he refused to let go of her voice for fear of losing her again.

"Will he always be this way, mistress?" Andrei asked.

"Hopefully, Andrei. The alternative is he remembers what he became, which would be a tragedy, or he becomes what he was, which I will not allow. Right now he is at peace with himself and no danger to anyone else."

"And the girl's family? Where's the justice for them?"

"Sometimes justice comes in strange forms. Dalnos will spend the rest of his life confined to a small cell. His whole life will depend on what he remembers and what he has forgotten. He did not deserve his childhood. Perhaps now he will have some of the happiness he never knew then. The girl's family will have their memories. Little comfort, I know. It seems ironic that memories are the only thing he and they have left."

Andrei nodded sadly.

"Are you ready to leave, mistress?"

"In a moment. Leave us now, please."

After he left, Yemaya watched Dalnos for a few minutes. The man sat quietly in his chair talking in a low voice, his hands folded on his lap.

"Dalnos?"

Looking up, Dalnos saw his mother standing near him.

"Mama? I've been good. I listen to what you tell me," he said quietly, hoping for her approval.

"I know, son. I've been here all along. You've been very good."

Dalnos smiled, pleased at her approval. His mother walked over and put her arms around him and rocked back and forth, holding him close.

"Dalnos, I have to leave for a while, but I'll still be here with you like I've always been. We'll talk like we've been doing. You just won't see me. Do you understand?"

Nodding, Dalnos hugged her tight.

"Yes, mama. Like before. When will I see you again?"

"Soon, my son. Listen to the people who are taking care of you, and if you need anything or to see me, ask for Andrei. Okay?"

"You won't leave me alone like before will you, mama?"

"No, I'll always be here to talk and listen to you, I promise. Now you must sleep. Do you want me to sing to you? Remember the song I would sing when you were a small boy?"

"Oh, yes, mama. Please?" he cried, clapping his hands excitedly.

Her voice was soft, gentle, and slightly husky. The song was an old Romanian verse that had been passed down from generation to generation. Dalnos lay down, closed his eyes, and drifted off to sleep, his mama's fingers stroking his hair as her voice soothed him into a peaceful slumber.

Yemaya watched him as he relaxed and fell asleep. The anger she felt for him had vanished once she had accepted his sickness. Shaking her head sadly, she couldn't imagine the terror he must have experienced at the hands of his father as a child. Yemaya left the cell a few moments later.

On the way back to the estate, she thought about the recent events in her life. She had almost been killed through the sabotage of one of her performances. That attempt, however, had brought Dakota into her life, then had almost gotten Dakota killed by the hired goons of an overly ambitious, power hungry publishing tycoon. Yemaya had taken care of the problem, thinking he may have also been involved in the Charleston incident. Now Yemaya had her doubts about his connection to it.

Dalnos, the pathetic madman, had killed a villager and almost raped and killed her lover because of a dark spirit named Intunecat. That brought her to the spirits. Since Dakota's entrance into her life, both of them had been inundated with the spirits of another realm. What was the commonality, she wondered, then swore under her breath.

"Dakota," she said. "From the very beginning, everything has been about her and me. She is my strength and my weakness. If we stay together, her life will always be in danger because of me. But without her, I am nothing, my life is nothing. There has got to be a solution."

"Did you say something, mistress?" Andrei asked.

"No, not really. Just take me home, Andrei, take me home."

Dakota, her love, her life, was waiting for her. For the moment, that was enough.

THE END

ABOUT THE AUTHOR

Fran Heckrotte lives in sunny South Carolina with her husband. Some of her interests include motorcycling, boogie boarding, scuba diving, gardening, and watergardening. She spent three years in Alaska enjoying hiking, camping, gold panning and working part time at a local ranch. After moving to the South to become a policewoman for five years, she left law enforcement to become a carpenter. Now she owns a property management company. As time permits, she likes to travel to Montreal, Canada, and South Beach Miami with her gal pals to enjoy the nightlife.

Other Intaglio Publications Titles

Accidental Love, by B. L. Miller, ISBN: 1-933113-11-1, Price: 18.15
What happens when love is based on deception? Can it survive discovering the truth?

Code Blue, by KatLyn, ISBN: 1-933113-09-X, Price: $16.95 - Thrown headlong into one of the most puzzling murder investigations in the Burgh's history, Logan McGregor finds that politics, corruption, money and greed aren't the only barriers she must break through in order to find the truth.

Counterfeit World, by Judith K. Parker, ISBN: 1-933113-32-4, Price: $15.25
The U.S. government has been privatized, religion has only recently been decriminalized, the World Government keeps the peace on Earth—when it chooses—and multi-world corporations vie for control of planets, moons, asteroids, and orbits for their space stations.

Crystal's Heart, by B. L. Miller & Verda Foster, ISBN: 1-933113-24-3, Price: $18.50 - Two women who have absolutely nothing in common, and yet when they become improbable housemates, are amazed to find they can actually live with each other. And not only live...

Gloria's Inn, by Robin Alexander, ISBN: 1-933113-01-4, Price: $14.95 - Hayden Tate suddenly found herself in a world unlike any other, when she inherited half of an inn nestled away on Cat Island in the Bahamas.

Graceful Waters, by B. L. Miller & Verda Foster, ISBN: 1-933113-08-1, Price: $17.25 - Joanna Carey, senior instructor at Sapling Hill wasn't looking for anything more than completing one more year at the facility and getting that much closer to her private dream, a small cabin on a quiet lake. She was tough, smart and she had a plan for her life.

Halls Of Temptation, by Katie P. Moore, ISBN: 978-1-933113-42-5, Price: $15.50 – A heartfelt romance that traces the lives of two young women from their teenage years into adulthood, through the struggles of maturity, conflict and love.

I Already Know The Silence Of The Storms, by N. M. Hill, ISBN: 1-933113-07-3, Price: $15.25 - I Already Know the Silence of the Storms is a map of a questor's journey as she traverses the tempestuous landscapes of heart, mind, body, and soul. Tossed onto paths of origins and destinations unbeknownst to her, she is enjoined by the ancients to cross chartless regions beset with want and need and desire to find the truth within.

Incommunicado, by N. M. Hill & J. P. Mercer, ISBN: 1-933113-10-3, Price: $15.25 - Incommunicado is a world of lies, deceit, and death along the U.S/Mexico border. Set within the panoramic beauty of the unforgiving Sonoran Desert, it is the story of two strong, independent women: Cara Vittore Cipriano, a lawyer who was born to rule the prestigious Cipriano Vineyards; and Jaquelyn "Jake" Biscayne, an FBI forensic pathologist who has made her work her life.

Infinite Pleasures, Stacia Seaman & Nann Dunne (Eds.), ISBN: 1-933113-00-6, Price: $18.99 - Hot, edgy, beyond-the-envelope erotica from over thirty of the best lesbian authors writing today. This no-holds barred, tell it like you wish it could be collection is guaranteed to rocket your senses into overload and ratchet your body up to high-burn.

Josie & Rebecca: The Western Chronicles, by Vada Foster & BL Miller, ISBN: 1-933113-38-3, Price: $18.99 - At the center of this story are two women; one a deadly gunslinger bitter from the injustices of her past, the other a gentle dreamer trying to escape the horrors of the present. Their destinies come together one fateful afternoon when the feared outlaw makes the choice to rescue a young woman in trouble. For her part, Josie Hunter considers the brief encounter at an end once the girl is safe, but Rebecca Cameron has other ideas....

Misplaced People, by C. G. Devize, ISBN: 1-933113-30-8, Price: $17.99 - On duty at a London hospital, American loner Striker West is drawn to an unknown woman, who, after being savagely attacked, is on the verge of death. Moved by a compassion she cannot explain, Striker spends her off time at the bedside of the comatose patient, reading and willing her to recover. Still trying to conquer her own demons which have taken her so far from home, Striker is drawn deeper into the web of intrigue that surrounds this woman.

Murky Waters, by Robin Alexander, ISBN: 1-933113-33-2, Price: $15.25 - Claire Murray thought she was leaving her problems behind when she accepted a new position within Suarez Travel and relocated to Baton Rouge. Her excitement quickly diminishes when her mysterious stalker makes it known that there is no place Claire can hide. She is instantly attracted to the enigmatic Tristan Delacroix, who becomes more of a mystery to her every time they meet. Claire is thrust into a world of fear, confusion, and passion that will ultimately shake the foundations of all she once believed.

None So Blind, by LJ Maas, ISBN: 978-1-933113-44-9, Price: $16.50 - Torrey Gray hasn't seen the woman she fell in love with in college for 15 years. Taylor Kent, now a celebrated artist, has spent the years trying to forget, albeit unsuccessfully, the young woman who walked out of Taylor's life…

Picking Up The Pace, by Kimberly LaFontaine, ISBN: 1-933113-41-3, Price: 15.50 - Who would have thought a 25-year-old budding journalist could stumble across a story worth dying for in quiet Fort Worth, Texas? Angie Mitchell certainly doesn't and neither do her bosses. While following an investigative lead for the Tribune, she heads into the seediest part of the city to discover why homeless people are showing up dead with no suspects for the police to chase.

Southern Hearts, by Katie P Moore, ISBN: 1-933113-28-6, Price: $16.95 - For the first time since her father's passing three years prior, Kari Bossier returns to the south, to her family's stately home on the emerald banks of the bayou Teche, and to a mother she yearns to understand.

Storm Surge, by KatLyn, ISBN: 1-933113-06-5, Price: $16.95 - FBI Special Agent Alex Montgomery would have given her life in the line of duty, but she lost something far more precious when she became the target of ruthless drug traffickers. Recalled to Jacksonville to aid the local authorities in infiltrating the same deadly drug ring, she has a secret agenda--revenge. Despite her unexpected involvement with Conner Harris, a tough, streetwise detective who has dedicated her life to her job at the cost of her own personal happiness, Alex vows to let nothing--and no one--stand in the way of exacting vengeance on those who took from her everything that mattered.

These Dreams, by Verda Foster, ISBN: 1-933113-12-X, Price: $15.75 - Haunted from childhood by visions of a mysterious woman she calls, Blue Eyes, artist Samantha McBride is thrilled when a friend informs her that she's seen a woman who bears the beautiful face she has immortalized on canvas and dreamed about for so long. Thrilled by the possibility that Blue Eyes might be a flesh and blood person, Samantha sets out to find her, certain the woman must be her destiny.

The Chosen, by Verda H Foster, ISBN: 978-1-933113-25-8, Price: 15.25 - animals. That's the way it's always been. But the slaves are waiting for the coming of The Chosen One, the prophesied leader who will take them out of their bondage.

The Cost Of Commitment, by Lynn Ames, ISBN: 1-933113-02-2, Price: $16.95 - Kate and Jay want nothing more than to focus on their love. But as Kate settles in to a new profession, she and Jay become caught up in the middle of a deadly scheme—pawns in a larger game in which the stakes are nothing less than control of the country.

The Gift, by Verda Foster, ISBN: 1-933113-03-0, Price: $15.35 - Detective Rachel Todd doesn't believe in Lindsay Ryan's visions of danger, even when the horrifying events Lindsay predicted come true. That mistake could cost more than one life before this rollercoaster ride is over. Verda Foster's The Gift is just that – a well-paced, passionate saga of suspense, romance, and the amazing bounty of family, friends, and second chances. From the first breathless page to the last, a winner.

The Last Train Home, by Blayne Cooper, ISBN: 1-933113-26-X, Price: $17.75 - One cold winter's night in Manhattan's Lower East side, tragedy strikes the Chisholm family. Thrown together by fate and disaster, Virginia "Ginny" Chisholm meets Lindsay Killian, a street-smart drifter who spends her days picking pockets and riding the rails. Together, the young women embark on a desperate journey that spans from the slums of New York City to the Western Frontier, as Ginny tries to reunite her family, regardless of the cost.

The Price of Fame, by Lynn Ames, ISBN: 1-933113-04-9, Price: $16.75 - When local television news anchor Katherine Kyle is thrust into the national spotlight, it sets in motion a chain of events that will change her life forever. Jamison "Jay" Parker is an intensely career-driven Time magazine reporter; she has experienced love once, from afar, and given up on finding it again...That is, until circumstance and an assignment bring her into contact with her past.

The Taking of Eden, by Robin Alexander, ISBN: 978-1-933113-53-1, Price: $15.95 - Frustrated with life and death situations that she can't control, Jamie Spencer takes a new job at a mental health facility, where she believes she can make a difference in her patients' lives. The difference she makes in Eden Carlton's life turns her world upside down and out of control. A spur-of-the-moment decision sets in motion a turn of events that she is powerless to stop and changes her life and everyone around her forever.

The Value of Valor, by Lynn Ames, ISBN: 1-933113-04-9, Price: $16.75
Katherine Kyle is the press secretary to the president of the United States. Her lover, Jamison Parker, is a respected writer for Time magazine. Separated by unthinkable tragedy, the two must struggle to survive against impossible odds...

The War between The Hearts, by Nann Dunne, ISBN: 1-933113-27-8, Price: $16.95 - Intent on serving the Union Army as a spy, Sarah-Bren Coulter disguises herself as a man and becomes a courier-scout for the Confederate Army. Soon the savagery of war shakes her to the core. She stifles her emotions so she can bear the guilt of sending men, and sometimes boys, into paths of destruction.

With Every Breath, by Alex Alexander, ISBN: 1-933113-39-1, Price: $15.25
Abigail Dunnigan wakes to a phone call telling her of the brutal murder of her former lover and dear friend. A return to her hometown for the funeral soon becomes a run for her life, not only from the murderer but also from the truth about her own well-concealed act of killing to survive during a war. As the story unfolds, Abby confesses her experiences in Desert Storm and becomes haunted with the past as the bizarre connection between then and now reveals itself. While the FBI works to protect her and apprehend the murderer, the murderer works to push Abby over the mental edge with their secret correspondence.

Intaglio Publication's Forthcoming Releases

Coming 2006

February
Romance for LIFE, Lori L. Lake & Tara Young, Eds, ISBN: 978-1-933113-59-3
Private Dancer, by T. J. Vertigo, ISBN: 978-1-933113-58-6
Define Destiny, by J. M. Dragon, ISBN: 1-933113-56-1
Journey's Of Discoveries, by Ellis Paris Ramsay, ISBN: 978-1-933113-43-2
Assignment Sunrise, by I Christie, ISBN: 978-1-933113-40-1

March
Prairie Fire, By LJ Maas, ISBN: 978-1-933113-47-0
Compensation, by S. Anne Gardner, ISBN: 978-1-933113-57-9

April
She Waits, by M. K. Sweeney, ISBN: 978-1-933113-55-5
Meridio's Daughter, By LJ Maas, ISBN: 978-1-933113-48-7
The Petal of the Rose, by LJ Maas, ISBN: 978-1-933113-49-4

May
Tumbleweed Fever, By LJ Maas, ISBN: 978-1-933113-51-7
The Scent of Spring, By Katie Moore, ISBN: 978-1-933113-67-8

June
Bloodlust, by Fran Heckrotte, ISBN: 978-1-933113-50-0
The Flipside of Desire, by Lynn Ames, ISBN: 978-1-933113-60-9

November
Times Fell Hand, By LJ Maas, ISBN: 978-1-933113-52-4